Benny held her g  to you? Don't tell me

She didn't, of course. wanted to believe in magic and pixie dust and happily ever after, but experience had taught her those things were for dreamers. In the real world, parents abandoned their children, marriages broke up, and adoptions fell through. Reality was hard, and magic was for fairy tales.

But it'd been Nick who reminded her that once upon a time she *had* believed.

She shrugged. "I remember a time not too long ago when I made a wish." She didn't like thinking about that time when it felt like there was nothing and no one who cared. But something about Benny's patient gaze made her want to tell him things she'd kept inside for too long, like how lost and alone she'd felt the day Nick—Santa—had asked her what she wanted for Christmas.

Just stick with the basics, she cautioned herself. Benny didn't need to know everything. "Santa granted my wish." She blinked a tear from her eye. "To me it was magic. Christmas magic." She shoved the box into his hand. "Maybe if you believe hard enough, wishes really can come true. What's the harm in trying?"

Benny smiled, and suddenly she saw him as more than just a man down on his luck. His smile was genuine, and his gaze sincere. "If it means that much to you," he said, "I'll make a Christmas wish."

"Promise?" Laura didn't know why it was important to her, but it was.

"I promise."

Praise for Linda Bleser

Reviewers have hailed Linda Bleser's work as unique, original, and impossible to put down. Her books have won several awards, including five EPPIE Awards, two Dream Realm Awards, the Dorothy Parker Reviewers Choice Award, The Royal Palm Literary Award, and several readers' choice awards.

The Magic Christmas Box

by

Linda Bleser

The Magic Christmas Box

Cover Art by *Tina Lynn Stout*

The Wild Rose Press, Inc.
PO Box 708
Adams Basin, NY 14410-0708
Visit us at www.thewildrosepress.com

Publishing History
First Fantasy Rose Edition, 2020
Trade Paperback ISBN 978-1-5092-3236-9
Digital ISBN 978-1-5092-3237-6

Published in the United States of America

Dedication

This book is dedicated to everyone
who still holds the magic and mystery of Christmas
in your heart.
May all your wishes and dreams come true.

Chapter One

Funny how something as simple as a hot meal and a stranger's smile could make a man feel almost human again.

Benny had been living on ramen noodles and peanut butter for the last few weeks. He had to find a new job soon or he wouldn't be able to afford even that. The sign for a free Christmas Eve dinner at the community center had been posted on the bulletin board in the lobby of his apartment building for over a week. At first, he'd balked. He wasn't one of those people who needed assistance. But then his stomach growled, and he realized yes, he was.

At least temporarily.

He stepped inside the room, taking in the surroundings. It smelled like Christmas and cranberries. He was drawn to the tree in a corner. Scotch pine, the same kind of tree his family cut down every year for Christmas. It was decorated with mismatched ornaments and paper chains made from red and green construction paper. He tugged on a pine needle and pressed his thumbnail into the center, releasing the aroma. The scent took him back to his childhood, a roaring fire and presents under the tree. He blinked back sudden tears.

Overwhelmed by a sense of loneliness, he turned to

leave, when a man dressed in a Santa suit stepped close to him.

"Don't go." The words stopped him. Benny did a double take. This Santa looked like the real deal. From his authentic snow-white beard to his bifocal glasses, he looked exactly like every picture of Santa Claus on every Christmas card he ever recalled.

"I'm here for the children," he explained pointing out the red suit. "They come over from the shelter every year."

Benny glanced around at the children with their shy smiles and hand-me-down clothes.

"Their lives may not be perfect," the man said, "but they're always happy to see Santa and get a candy cane and a hug."

Benny nodded. "I was just—"

"I know. You were about to leave. But I think you should stay."

As he talked, he gently guided Benny toward the food line. "No one should be alone for the holidays. And I hear the turkey is especially tasty this year."

The aroma of turkey and gravy was all the motivation Benny needed. He decided to stay after all.

The man in the Santa suit tilted his head. "Coffee and cider on the table over there. Help yourself."

"I will." Benny held out his hand. "Thank you."

"My pleasure." The man took Benny's hand and gave it a firm shake, then glanced at his watch. "Time to get to work. Enjoy your meal and stick around. I might have a little something for you as well." He winked, then turned and walked away.

"I'm a little old for coloring books," Benny said. "But I wouldn't turn down a candy cane."

"One candy cane coming right up." The man smiled, then turned and walked back across the room to a make-shift Santa throne where several children waited patiently.

Benny took his place in line with the homeless and forgotten, while women wearing hair nets piled food onto his plate. He found a seat at a long wooden table. His dish overflowed with all the Christmas trimmings—turkey, mashed potatoes, stuffing and gravy, with cranberry sauce on the side and a biscuit balanced on top. The aroma made his mouth water.

He ate slowly, savoring each bite. Christmas carols played softly in the background, mingling with the sound of children laughing as they took turns sitting on Santa's lap. Benny's mood lightened. He was glad the man in the red suit convinced him to stay.

A tow-headed boy plopped his dish on the table then climbed onto the chair across from Benny. "Hi."

"Hi." Benny looked around for a parent or guardian, but there was no adult in sight.

"What's your name?' the boy asked.

"Benny." Still no sign of anyone.

The boy giggled and covered his mouth.

"What's so funny?"

"Bunny like the Easter Bunny?"

Benny couldn't help but smile back. "No, Benny. Like a penny."

For some reason the boy found that even funnier. He giggled, this time exposing two missing teeth. "Hi Benny like a penny."

"Hi, um…what's your name?"

"Gabe. Gabriel Alexander Watson."

Benny nodded. "That's a lot of name for a young

boy."

"My mom told me I'll grow into it." Gabe patted the bib of his denim overalls. "Like these clothes. I got them when I was four and a half and now I'm five and all growed into them."

"Moms are smart that way." Benny looked around. "Speaking of mothers, where's yours? And didn't she tell you not to talk to strangers?"

The boy's smile faded. "I don't live with her anymore."

Benny's heart sank. How could he have been so thoughtless? Hadn't the man playing Santa mentioned the kids came from the shelter? Before opening his big mouth, Benny should have realized the boy didn't have a traditional family life.

"Miss Laura brought us here," Gabe said. "She went to the room for ladies and told me not to move, but I did because that table had a snow man on it and this table has Santa Claus, and I love Santa Claus more than anything else." He spooned some cranberry sauce into his mouth, then pointed to Benny's dish. "Are you gonna eat your cookie?"

"Nope. Want it?"

"I'll trade you for my green beans."

Benny patted his stomach. "No thanks. I ate all my green beans already," he said, slipping the cookie onto Gabe's plate. "I'm stuffed."

****

How hard could it be to chaperone a few kids for an hour or so? Inexperienced though she was with children, Laura Lee Bell thought volunteering at the shelter would be a piece of cake. She'd been unprepared for the energetic exuberance of the boys and the clingy, neediness of the girls. Six of them, each demanding her complete attention in their own sticky-fingered way.

It started out well enough. She'd lined them up for their visits with Santa, herding them back into line when needed. She'd just gotten the kids settled at the lunch table when seven-year old Prissy started screaming that she had to go to the bathroom. Laura looked around for one of the other chaperones, but Prissy's screams intensified to an ear-splitting level.

"Don't anyone move from this table," she ordered the children. At their combined nods, she'd hurried Prissy to the girls' room. When she returned, she counted heads, only to discover one tow-headed boy missing.

Where is...?

She caught sight of Gabe across the room talking to a dark-haired stranger, and her heart lurched. She grabbed the arm of Carol Miller, one of the social workers at the shelter. "Watch them for a minute please. I have to round up an escaped orphan."

Carol nodded and Laura rushed across the room.

"Gabe! I told you to stay over there with the other children."

The boy's bottom lip jutted out. "I didn't like it over there."

She turned her back to the man at the table and leaned close, whispering in Gabe's ear.

"He's not a stranger," Gabe shouted. "His name is Benny Penny and he's Santa's friend. I saw them talking."

Laura let out a slow sigh, torn between keeping her charge safe and letting him believe in the magic of

Christmas for a little while longer.

"It's okay," the man said. "You're both welcome to sit here."

"Thank you, Mr. Penny, but…"

"It's just Benny, ma'am. And there's a good chance I can get Santa to come over to the table when he's done for a little one-on-one chat with the boy."

Gabe tugged on the woman's sleeve. "Please, Miss Laura. Please?"

She gave him an indulgent smile, then shot Benny a look that warned him not to betray her trust. It was hard to stay angry when his quick smile transformed him from dangerous stranger to innocent charmer. Finally, she took a seat beside Gabe. "Okay, young man. You can stay on one condition. You have to eat all your beans."

Gabe looked down at his plate, seeming to weigh the options. A personal visit from Santa won. "Okay." He shoved a forkful of green beans into his mouth and talked around them. "Did you tell Santa what you wanted for Christmas Mr. Benny?"

"Not yet," Benny replied. "I was waiting for my turn."

Gabe pointed to where Santa sat on the other side of the room. "You have to wait in line for about four hundred minutes. Then when it's your turn you tell Santa what you want, he gives you a coloring book and a candy cane." He glanced up, his little legs kicking back and forth on the chair. "Right Miss Laura?"

She brushed the bangs from his forehead. "That's right."

"I asked Santa for dinosaur stuff and Legos and books."

Benny quirked an eyebrow. "You can read?"

"No, but I'm learning to read in kindergarten. I'm learning to make my letters. I can make a G. Want to see?"

Before Benny could answer, the boy drew the letter G in his mashed potatoes with his index finger. "G for Gabe," he announced proudly, then sucked the potatoes off his finger.

"That's a good G." Benny turned to Laura and smiled. "Wouldn't you say?"

Before she could reply, a little girl rushed up and tugged on her blouse. "Miss Laura, Jeremy took my candy cane and he won't give it back."

Laura glanced from Gabe to the girl and back.

"Don't worry," Benny said. "He'll be fine with me. We'll practice our letters together."

She gave him a long, hard stare, but the girl's frenzied cries won out. "I'll be right back," she told Gabe, then turned her gaze back to Benny. "I'll be over there where I can see you."

Benny was momentarily stunned by smoky gray eyes that hinted at hidden secrets like valleys layered in fog. He was struck by a desire to delve deep beneath the misty haze and uncover the mysteries hidden behind them.

He attempted a sincere and disarming smile. "We'll be right here," he assured her. "Waiting for Santa to come over." He gestured across the room. "Here he comes now." His voice softened. "No need to worry."

She glanced across the room and saw her old friend Nick heading toward the table. Whether it was Benny's heartfelt assurance or the fact that they'd have a jolly old chaperone, she knew Gabe would be safe with his new friend.

When Laura left, Gabe turned to Benny with wide-eyed wonder. "Do you really know Santa Claus?"

"Well, I just met him today."

"Me too." Gabe leaned forward and whispered, "He's magic, you know."

"So I've heard."

"He can fly with his reindeers and stuff, and he has elves, and they make presents for every boy and girl in the whole world." He drew out the word *whole* with dramatic flair.

"Wow."

Gabe nodded his head up and down rapidly. "That's like four hundred presents."

Four hundred seemed to be Gabe's favorite number. He was about to ask if Gabe could count that high but was afraid of the answer. He'd like to be home before dark.

Benny noticed Laura speaking to the man in the Santa suit. He whispered something to her, and she nodded then continued on her way, but not before looking back and giving Benny a warning glare.

The man playing Santa came over to the table. "So, Gabe," he said. "I see you met my friend Benny."

Gabe nodded his head up and down, seemingly awe-struck in front of his hero. Benny tried to remember if he'd introduced himself to the man in the red suit. He must have. How else would he know his name?

Unless he really was Santa Claus.

Benny smiled at his own foolishness. It was one thing to be an impressionable five-year old, but Benny was old enough to know better.

Santa turned his attention to Benny. "Seems I have a gift with your name on it." He set a box wrapped in silver foil and tied with a red ribbon on the table.

"Open it, open it," Gabe cried.

Benny looked at the man in the red suit, who nodded. "Go ahead. Open it."

A present was the last thing Benny expected. He hadn't even put up a tree this year. There was no one to share the joy of the season with. "I couldn't…"

"Of course, you can." Santa placed a hand over Benny's. "Sometimes the best gifts are the unexpected ones. Go ahead and open it."

Benny moved his dinner tray out of the way and tugged on one end of the ribbon, untying the red bow, then slid a thumb beneath the wrapper, revealing a polished wooden box. Green garland with red holly berries were painted around the lid's border. Twinkling lights reflected off the surface of a metal plate attached to the front of the box. Benny rubbed his thumb over the metal and blinked. He leaned closer and read the name engraved on the plate.

Benjamin.

How…? He glanced at Santa who merely shrugged and smiled.

Benny shook his head. He felt a scam coming on but couldn't imagine what it might be. He flipped the ornamental latch and opened the lid. Red velvet lined the interior. It smelled like Christmas and cedar. A small notepad, along with a pen shaped like a candy cane, was nestled inside the box. Benny shot a quizzical glance at the man in the Santa suit.

"It's a wishing box," he said. "A magical

Christmas wishing box."

Benny raised an eyebrow. "A box that grants wishes?" He made a huffing sound. Magic didn't exist, but one look at the wonder in Gabe's eyes kept him from saying it out loud.

"If you don't believe me," the man said, "then what harm will come in giving it a try. Of course, if you don't take it seriously, you'll waste one of your three wishes."

"Why are there always three wishes?" Benny asked, hearing the skepticism in his own voice.

"That's just the way it is." Santa nudged the box closer to Benny. "Give it a try. What's the worst that can happen?"

Benny shrugged. That was true enough. Things couldn't get much worse.

Gabe reached out a finger toward the box. "Can I touch it?" His voice was a hushed whisper.

Santa and Benny both nodded.

Gabe brushed his finger over the polished wood, as gently as he might pet a newborn kitten. For a moment the box seemed to glow, but Benny figured it was probably a trick of the light.

"There are a few rules," Santa pointed out. He held up an index finger. "First. Write your wish down on the paper and place it in the box at midnight on Christmas Eve. The gift will arrive on your doorstep Christmas morning."

"Okay." Benny humored the man, but part of him wanted to hear what came next. "So, I make three wishes on Christmas Eve and…"

"No. You make your first wish on Christmas Eve."

"Only the first? What about the other two?"

The man in the Santa suit smiled. "You can only make the next wish once your previous wish is fulfilled. Wishes take time to develop. If you don't know what's lacking in your life, how do you know what to wish for next?"

Benny figured he could name three things right off the bat that he could wish for, but who was he to argue with magic?

Santa continued, counting off on each finger. "Second, your wish must be for yourself exclusively. It must be something *you* want."

Benny shrugged one shoulder. "I can live with that."

"And it can't be something ambiguous like world peace. Although that's a noble wish, it's impossible to grant and can't fit on your doorstep."

Benny wasn't sure if that was a joke or not, but since he had no intention of making any wishes, let alone three of them, it didn't matter. He was just playing along. "And the third rule?"

"That's easy. After your last wish is granted, the box must be returned. It can't be passed on to a friend or family member."

"That's it?"

"That's it. Three rules, three wishes, three gifts. That's the way it works."

Benny shook his head and pushed the box away. "If you say so."

Santa slid it back across the table and held Benny's gaze for a long moment. "What would you wish for if you *did* believe in magic?"

Benny thought about it. What does every man wish for? Security, of course. "A steady income, a fulfilling job, food on the table, good friends I can count on."

"Those are all good wishes."

"Assuming I believed in magic," Benny argued.

"The box doesn't care if you believe or not. It will grant your wishes either way." He tapped his finger on the lid. "Trust the box, Benny. It will always give you what you need."

The child inside Benny wanted to believe. Needed to believe. "One more thing," he said. "You didn't tell me your name."

The man glanced at the boy, then back to Benny. "Santa Claus, of course." He winked. "But you can call me Nick."

Nick took Gabe's hand. "Let's get you back to your group before Miss Laura has a conniption."

"What's a conniption?"

Nick chuckled. "It's when someone gets nervous and acts all crazy."

Gabe nodded, his voice soft. "I think my mom had a conniption."

Nick put his arm around the boy's shoulder and gave him a gentle hug.

****

Across the room Laura watched Nick interact with Benny and Gabe. If there was one person in the entire world whose opinion she trusted, it was Nick. She watched him give Gabe a hug, then lead him across the room to her table. The other children gathered around, clamoring for Santa's attention. He spoke to each one individually, then pulled Laura aside.

"You don't have to worry about Benny," he said. "He's one of the good guys.

"I wasn't worried about him. I didn't want to leave

Gabe alone with a stranger, let alone some homeless…"

"Benny's not homeless. Just temporarily down on his luck. But that's going to change. You'll see."

Laura glanced across the room at Benny. Shoulders slumped and head bowed, he looked more than down on his luck. He looked like someone who'd given up hope. She knew what that felt like.

Gabe tugged on her sleeve. "Santa gave Benny a magic box."

Laura smiled. "Oh?"

"Yep. It's magic, and he gets three wishes."

Laura knelt and held Gabe's gaze. "Three wishes, huh? What would you wish for if you had three wishes?"

Gabe chewed on his lower lip, then without hesitation recited, "I'd wish for a mom and a dad and a puppy."

Laura nodded. "Those are good wishes." She stood and patted Gabe on the back. "Now go get your jacket on, it's time to go." She turned away and brushed a tear from her eye.

Nick gave her a knowing look. It always made Laura smile to see Nick dressed up in his Santa costume. She was accustomed to his farmer's uniform of a flannel shirt and overalls. Either way, he couldn't disguise the ever-present twinkle in his sky-blue eyes. She reached out and gave him an impulsive hug. "Magic, huh?"

He took a slow, deep breath. "You used to believe in magic."

"That was a long time ago."

"No." Nick shook his head. "Not so long ago. You're still the strong, determined girl I remember.

Always looking on the bright side, no matter how dark it gets."

Laura turned aside. Maybe that's the way it looked to the rest of the world, but she'd been crying on the inside.

Nick pulled her attention back. "How's Edna doing?" he asked.

The thought of Edna brought a smile to her face. "She has good days and bad days. I'm sure she'd love to see you."

"I'll drop in. Maybe I'll bring her some of her favorite chocolate."

"She'd love that."

Nick looked around, a frown on her face. "Things aren't the same since…"

"I know," Laura agreed. "I know."

Only then did she notice Benny across the room. He turned to leave, but the box Nick had given him still rested on the table. Laura remembered when she was about Gabe's age she'd asked Santa for something special. She glanced at Nick, who smiled as if reading her mind, then jerked his head in Benny's direction.

The children had gathered around Carol, getting into their coats and boots. Without a second thought, Laura rushed across the room. She picked up the box and headed outside where she saw Benny walking away, his collar turned up against the cold.

"Benny," she called. "You forgot this."

He turned and gave her a questioning look. "It's just a box."

"A magic box," she said, catching up to him. "Nick wanted you to have it for a reason." If Nick said there was magic inside, she believed him. He had a way of making magical things happen.

"Well, I don't believe in magic. Magic is for children."

"Maybe, but maybe magic is something as simple as setting goals and intentions."

Benny held her gaze for a long moment. "What's it to you? Don't tell me you believe in this foolishness."

She didn't, of course. She wanted to believe in magic and pixie dust and happily ever after, but experience had taught her those things were for dreamers. In the real world, parents abandoned their children, marriages broke up, and adoptions fell through. Reality was hard, and magic was for fairy tales.

But it'd been Nick who reminded her that once upon a time she *had* believed.

She shrugged. "I remember a time not too long ago when I made a wish." She didn't like thinking about that time when it felt like there was nothing and no one who cared. But something about Benny's patient gaze made her want to tell him things she'd kept inside for too long, like how lost and alone she'd felt the day Nick—Santa—had asked her what she wanted for Christmas.

Just stick with the basics, she cautioned herself. Benny didn't need to know everything. "Santa granted my wish." She blinked a tear from her eye. "To me it was magic. Christmas magic." She shoved the box into his hand. "Maybe if you believe hard enough, wishes really can come true. What's the harm in trying?"

Benny smiled, and suddenly she saw him as more than just a man down on his luck. His smile was genuine, and his gaze sincere. "If it means that much to you," he said, "I'll make a Christmas wish."

"Promise?" Laura didn't know why it was important to her, but it was.

"I promise."

Now that she was sure he'd keep his promise, she said goodbye, turned, and walked back inside.

****

That evening Benny sat alone at his kitchen table, the box open in front of him. He felt foolish, but eventually gave in to the urge and pulled a piece of paper out of the box. He twirled the candy-cane pen, then tapped the pen on the paper. Why not? It wasn't as if he really believed in magic.

But if there was magic, he'd wish for a job. A good job. Not that his last job wasn't good. After accepting a promotion with a big department store chain, he'd moved to Sun Valley, Vermont. The town was charming, with its quaint colonials, antique shops and covered bridges, but before Benny could put down roots the company went bankrupt, catching everyone by surprise. Overnight, they closed their doors, leaving hundreds out of work, taking pensions and benefits with it.

If he had to wish for a new job, he'd wish big. Maybe he'd wish to be the CEO of some big international company. With a corner office. And benefits. And a retirement program. Benny wrote down all the things he'd want in this fictional dream job, turning the paper over when he ran out of space. When he was done, he put the wish in the box, waited until the clock struck midnight, closed the lid, and fastened the golden clasp.

There. Done.

Even while he chided himself for being foolish, a flare of something welled up inside him. Something he hadn't felt in a long time.

Hope.

After turning out the lights, he fell into bed and dreamed the dreams of innocence, none of which he remembered the next morning.

Chapter Two

Laura slipped out of bed at six o'clock Christmas morning, wide awake. The coffee pot was set to automatic, so all she had to do was pour her first cup of the day, open her laptop and scroll through her email.

She couldn't concentrate. Her thoughts kept coming back to the man she'd met at the community center. Benny. Even his name felt harmless. Not Ben or Benjamin, but good old Benny—your childhood friend or cheerful neighbor. She wondered if he'd kept his promise to put a wish inside the Christmas box. If so, had his wish come true? She shook her head, pushing thoughts of him aside and went back to answering email.

Half an hour later, she stood and stretched, then closed her laptop. Enough for now. She poured a second cup of coffee and carried it into the living room where a five-foot tree trimmed in red and gold took up half the space. She hit a switch and hundreds of twinkling lights glowed, bringing a smile to Laura's face. This was hers. All hers. And no one could take it away.

She couldn't help remembering years ago when a younger Nick had asked her what she wanted Santa to bring her. "A dress-up fashion doll," she'd whispered, knowing it was too much to ask for. But that Christmas morning the doll—along with an assortment of outfits, shoes and tiny plastic purses—showed up at the foot of her bed.

Once upon a time, Santa made her believe in magic and dreams and unspoken wishes. She still wanted to believe, but her years at Hyatt House changed that. There were no such things as miracles, and magic didn't exist.

The doll that Nick had given her for Christmas all those years ago, no longer dressed in dime-store clothes, today sat beneath the tree, wearing a fur-trimmed velvet Christmas outfit Laura lovingly dressed her in every year. It was a perennial reminder that Christmas wishes could sometimes come true.

A knock at the door pulled Laura out of her reverie. She opened the door to see Carol Miller holding up a bag of donuts. "I knew you'd be up early," she said. "Probably on your second cup of coffee already, right?"

Laura nodded and smiled.

Carol handed her the donuts. "I wanted to thank you for helping out with the kids yesterday. I know it isn't easy for you to return there."

Laura shrugged. Carol was right. It wasn't easy, but she'd put her past behind her for the most part. "It was nice to see Nick. Does he still deliver eggs to the shelter?"

"Every single Saturday," Carol replied.

Just as Laura remembered. In addition to playing Santa every Christmas, Nick had delivered four dozen fresh eggs from his farm to the shelter every Saturday, which the cook used to bake a week's worth of cakes, muffins and bread, leaving enough for Sunday breakfast.

After placing the donuts on a plate, she poured Carol a cup of coffee. They sat together at the kitchen table while Laura picked at her donut, breaking it into crumbling pieces.

Carol leaned forward. "I know things are different there now."

Laura shrugged. Different yes, but not necessarily better. Carol was part of the new regime, however, so Laura kept her opinion to herself.

Carol broke a chocolate donut in half. "What are your plans for today?"

The question was innocent enough, but Laura felt a sharp tug at her heart. Christmas didn't have the same memories for her as other people. There were no family traditions, no Christmas cookie recipes passed down from one generation to the next, no memories of Christmas trees laden with brightly wrapped gifts.

"I'll be going to the assisted living center, today," she said. "To visit Edna."

Carol gave a knowing nod. Everyone knew who Edna was. Edna B. Hyatt, founder of Hyatt House—the very same shelter where Laura had spent most of her life. "Well, to be honest," Carol said. "The donuts were not just a thank-you, but a bit of a bribe."

Laura raised a questioning eyebrow.

"It's Gabe. He's worried about you. He thinks you're sick."

"Sick?"

Carol smiled. "He said something about a conniption. I told him that was just a phrase, but he wants to see for himself that you're okay."

Laura couldn't help but chuckle. "Sounds like something Nick would say. But yes, even without the donuts I'll be happy to drop by and assure Gabe that I'm fine."

****

The forecasters had predicted a white Christmas, but there was no sign of snow outside his bedroom window. Benny slipped his bare feet into fleece-lined slippers and wrapped a flannel robe around his pajamas. He put coffee on to brew and stared out the window. There was always something magical about Christmas morning. Enchanting and filled with promise, it brought out the child inside. He remembered racing his brothers and sisters downstairs with squeals of delight when they spotted the gaily-wrapped presents piled neatly under the tree. They weren't allowed to touch the gifts until their parents came down, but they could check their stockings, unloading candy and apples, socks and playing cards. The treasures held them over until they could unwrap their Christmas gifts.

Benny took his time preparing coffee. He spooned sugar into his cup and stirred, all the while avoiding glancing at the front door. He sat down and opened his laptop. Social media was filled with pictures of families dressed in matching Christmas pajamas and people celebrating at parties, making Benny feel even more alone. His brothers and sisters were scattered across the country now, busy with careers and families. The last time they'd all been together was two years ago. This year he couldn't even afford a plane ticket to visit his parents in Florida. He'd have to settle for video chats with his nieces and nephews, but that wasn't the same as being there in person. As for friends, he hadn't been in town long enough to meet anyone but his next-door neighbor. After the store closed, even his co-workers had scattered, seeking employment opportunities in neighboring towns.

The minutes ticked by and soon the urge to peek outside the front door became too hard to ignore. He didn't have a front porch, just a step into a hallway that smelled like dust and old cabbage. Benny vowed one of the first things he'd do once he got a job was find a better place to live.

A job.

That was all he could think about from the moment he'd climbed out of bed. If he could believe the box really granted wishes, what would he find waiting on his doorstep? Maybe a letter from one of the many places he'd applied requesting an interview? Or perhaps a newspaper with the perfect job listed at the top of the Help Wanted section. He shrugged. The only way to find out was to open the door.

He gripped the handle and turned, preparing to be disappointed. The doorknob was cold in his palm and at first refused to turn. At last it slid into place, and Benny opened it. He looked down to see a fruitcake covered in clear plastic wrap sitting squarely on his welcome mat.

A fruitcake?

Only then did he notice the fruitcake was perched atop a slender package wrapped in silver foil with a shiny red bow. He knelt and picked them both up, turning the package from one side to the other.

Cradling both to his chest, Benny went inside and closed the door behind him. He almost wished he had a Christmas tree so he could set the present under it and bask in child-like delight. But he didn't have a tree, or even an ornament of any kind to celebrate the season, so he set the present on the table and simply stared, almost afraid to unwrap it and be disappointed.

Instead, he focused on the fruitcake. Not necessarily a favorite of his, but it brought back memories. His grandmother baked fruitcake every Christmas, and once he was old enough, she let him help in the kitchen. The smell of baking was inextricably tied to the holiday season.

He poured a fresh cup of coffee and checked the label—*Magical Fruit Cake from Beverley's Bake Shop*. The ingredients were listed on the label, including something called cinnamon sugar pixie dust. Odd, but Benny figured any bakery that called its fruitcake magical would also claim it was sprinkled with pixie dust. It made sense in a whimsical kind of way.

He unwrapped the fruitcake and cut a thick slice. He could almost see the smile on his grandmother's face when, as a young boy, he picked out the little green fruits in her fruitcake. This fruitcake was different, however. It was dense, loaded with nuts and fresh fruit as opposed to the little gummy chunks in the ones he remembered. The sweetness of the cake was a delightful contrast to the strong coffee. Pixie dust or no pixie dust, it was a great start to Christmas day.

Finally, Benny's curiosity got the better of him. He pulled the present across the table, tugged on one end of the ribbon, and the bow slid free. He held his breath and slipped a finger under the folded edge, finally revealing what lay beneath the silver foil.

A notebook. It was as meaningless and unexpected as the fruitcake. Maybe they were for someone else and had accidentally found their way to his front door. Maybe they were meant for Mrs. Sobieski across the hall?

Curious, he opened the book. It was a simple dime-store notebook, the kind kids bought for their first day of school. Someone had written LOVE YOUR JOB at the top of the first page in bold black marker, followed by a list. The rules—*Why were there always rules?*—were simple. Fill each page. No one-word answers allowed. Each page began with a question. The rest of the page was blank.

Finishing up the slice of fruitcake, Benny pushed his dish aside and flipped through the pages of the notebook, intrigued by the cryptic questions.

Indoor or Outdoor?
People or Paper?
Save or Spend?
Today or Tomorrow?
Strengths and Skills?
Leader or Follower?
Introvert or Extrovert?

Further into the book the questions delved deeper. What were his talents, his likes, his skills, his long-range goals? What made him feel happy? At the back of the book was a sample resume to fill out based on the answers to his questions.

Some of the questions seemed simple at first, but once he started writing, he uncovered things about himself he hadn't expected. Would answering these questions lead him to a perfect job?

Trust the box.

Was it a coincidence that he'd wished for a job and received a journal about finding the right job for him? It would have been easy for his mysterious friend Nick to put the package on his doorstep, and it wouldn't take a rocket scientist to figure out he'd wish for a job. He even recalled mentioning it when they'd talked.

Benny was almost halfway through the notebook when he realized what he'd always believed was his "dream job" was not the job for him. What he really wanted was to work outdoors with people, not cooped up in an office.

He glanced at the clock, surprised to find that several hours had passed. In that time Benny developed a greater understanding of what he was looking for. *Could it be this simple?* Had he been applying for jobs he wasn't suited for—jobs that would simply have made him miserable in the long run?

He stood and stretched the kinks from his back, then cut several slices of fruitcake and put them in a plastic container. He went across the hall and knocked on Mrs. Sobieski's door.

"Benjamin," she said in greeting, wiping her hands on a checkered dish cloth. She was dressed for the season in green pants and a sparkly red sweater with tiny jeweled Christmas trees dangling from her ears. Red and green bows adorned her gray hair.

"Merry Christmas, Mrs. Sobieski." He held out the container. "I brought you some fruitcake. I hope you like it."

"That was very thoughtful of you. Come." she waved him in. "Come inside."

Benny followed her into her apartment, surprised to see a table-top Christmas tree in the living room. Decorations covered every surface, and Christmas cards were strung along the walls, as high as Mrs. Sobieski's five-foot nothing height could reach.

"I was going to stop by later today," she said. "But since you're here anyway you might as well take these now." She pointed to a covered plate of Christmas cookies. "Made them myself. I love to bake, but now that the kids are grown and moved away, I can't have all these sweets in my house. Not with my diabetes, anyway. So, I make them for my bridge club. And neighbors."

"I appreciate it, Mrs. Sobieski."

"Call me Sally." She pointed to a kitchen chair. "Have a seat. I always keep some cookies aside for company. You're company," she added with a smile. "Would you like milk or tea with them?"

Benny was about to tell her not to bother, but they were both alone on Christmas Day, so why not? Besides, the cookies looked delicious. "Milk, please."

She nodded, placed a dish of cookies in front of him, and then turned to the refrigerator to get the milk. It was ice cold and the perfect accompaniment to his neighbor's sweet treats.

Mrs. Sobieski—Sally—sat across from him, elbows on the table, chin resting on her folded hands. She watched every bite that went into his mouth, as if eating the cookie vicariously through him. "Good?"

Benny swallowed and nodded. "Delicious. These ones here…"

"Thumbprint cookies. You press your thumb in the cookie before baking it, and then fill the indentation with jam."

"Yeah. My mother used to make them. They were my favorite."

"Mine too." She drummed her fingers on the desk. "I'm guessing you didn't bake that fruitcake."

"Nope. But I have dabbled under my grandmother's guidance."

She grinned. "So, where did it come from?"

Benny shrugged. "A place called Beverley's Bake Shop. It supposedly has magical properties." He left out the part about the pixie dust.

"Oh," Sally said. "I've been to that bakery. Beverley is a lovely woman, and if I'm not mistaken, she also prepares sweets for the children at the shelter. Who bought it for you?"

"I'm pretty sure it's a gift left on my doorstep from someone who wants me to believe he's Santa Claus."

Sally stopped tugging on the plastic wrap and frowned at Benny. "Why would he do that?"

"I don't know exactly." Benny told her about meeting the man who played Santa and the magic box. "He left a book as well."

She waited with an expectant look on her face, making it easier for him to talk about it. "Funny, according to the book, I've been applying for jobs in all the wrong places. This book is about searching inside yourself to find the job that's made for you, not the job you think you want." He frowned. "It's hard to explain."

"Not hard at all. You know what they say, *Find a job you love and you will never have to work a day in your life.*"

"Confucius?"

She shrugged one shoulder. "Or Mr. Rogers. One or the other."

Benny couldn't help smiling with her. "Well, I learned a lot about myself. Turns out I'm not suited to sitting behind a desk or being in an office all day. I'll be happier working with people, possibly outdoors."

Sally tilted her head and pursed her lips. "Like

maybe a country club or something?"

Benny thought about it. "Sure, that would work. Why?"

Sally tapped a finger to her lips. "My friend Judy from the bridge club mentioned her nephew is looking for someone to work at Sun Valley Country Club. He's the manager there. I wasn't really paying much attention because it was my turn to bid, but I could find out if the job is still available and how much—"

"It doesn't matter how much the pay is," Benny interrupted. "I'll take anything."

"No, you won't," she reprimanded. "You'll take the job that makes you happy. The job you can't wait to get to when you wake up in the morning."

"Ahh…Mr. Rogers?"

"No. That was just me."

He reached out and placed his hand over hers. "Thank you. For the cookies and milk, and for the company."

"You're welcome." She handed him the covered dish of cookies with his name on it, then walked him to the door. "Merry Christmas, Benjamin."

He left feeling lighter than when he came in. The Christmas spirit, which had eluded him up until now, cast a cheery holiday glow around everything.

Chapter Three

Sun Valley Assisted Living was bright, clean, and cheerful. The walls were painted in relaxing tones of gray, and the hallways were covered in a padded laminate, making walker and wheelchair navigation easier and more forgiving of bumps and spills.

When Laura stopped at the desk, the receptionist greeted her by name since she was a frequent visitor. Edna's apartment was like all the others, but there were personal touches that made it hers alone—the Longaberger basket filled with her needlepoint, the Princess Diana commemorative tea set on her counter, and the crocheted doilies draped over the armrests of her recliner.

Edna gave her a warm, welcoming hug. "Merry Christmas, my dear."

Laura wrapped her arms around the older woman, closed her eyes and inhaled Edna's familiar gardenia scent. When Edna founded Hyatt House, she took the time to make a special connection with each and every child who came through the doors. She was the closest thing Laura had to a mother figure. Edna had taken Laura under her wing, took her shopping for her first bra and helped her apply for scholarships and grants that, along with several part-time jobs, allowed Laura to get a two-year business degree.

"I brought you a present," Laura said, handing Edna a wrapped package.

"Oh, you shouldn't have, dear." Edna wasted little time as she tore the paper off and exclaimed when she saw the box of assorted chocolates—her favorite.

"I know you love them." Plus, it was the one thing Edna allowed Laura to buy for her, proclaiming she didn't need anything at her age. The assisted living center provided everything she needed, from meals to cleaning services to 24-hour nursing care.

Edna opened the lid and held the box out to Laura. "Would you like one, dear?"

"No thank you." Laura knew Edna would treasure the chocolate, savoring one individual piece each evening after watching her favorite television game show.

Edna carried the box to a floral-patterned couch and patted the cushion, inviting Lauren to join her. "How are things at Hyatt House?" She always asked, and Laura always tried to sugar-coat her answer.

Hyatt House was Edna's baby. She'd given it everything she'd had for most of her life. Then she'd gotten sick and the medical bills had piled up. Edna had held out as long as she could, but eventually was forced to sell Hyatt House to a faceless corporation. Suddenly there were new rules and new regulations. Hyatt House still carried her name, but without Edna at the helm, the heart and soul was missing.

"I'm going over there, later today," Laura said. "There's a little boy who's captured my heart."

"More than one, I bet." Edna squeezed Laura's hand. "You have a big heart. I'm sure you'd adopt them all if you could."

"If I could," Laura admitted, knowing it wasn't a possibility, mostly because one of the new rules in place at Hyatt House prohibited single parents from adopting. Edna believed, with her whole heart, that every child deserved to be loved, whether by a single parent, a mixed-race couple, or a same-sex family. Placing children in loving homes was not only her dream, but her life's work.

Laura believed Hyatt House had taken a step backward under new management, and she did everything she could to shield Edna from finding out what had become of her dream.

Edna patted Laura's hand. "I have something for you."

With great effort, she pushed herself to her feet and trudged slowly across the room, leaning heavily on her cane. She opened a jewelry box, took something out, and then returned to where Laura waited. Edna took a deep breath, then opened her hand to reveal a beautiful antique diamond ring.

Laura drew back. "Oh, I couldn't."

"Of course, you can, dear. I can't wear it anymore with the arthritis, and besides, I want you to have it." She pushed the ring onto Laura's finger. "Mr. Hyatt put that on my finger fifty-two years ago. It represents all the happiness I wish for you."

The ring fit perfectly. Its shine magnified by the tears in Laura's eyes. "Thank you," she said.

Edna nodded. "You're the closest thing I have to a daughter. If I hadn't gotten sick…"

Laura had been fourteen when Edna filed adoption papers. She thought she'd burst with happiness. Finally. A family of her own. It was the one thing she'd been hoping and praying for. Then Edna got sick and everything fell apart. She reached out and gave Edna a warm hug. "It doesn't matter. Thank you. For everything."

"Someday a smart young man will put a real engagement ring on that finger. But until then, know that you are, and always will be, loved."

****

After Benny left Sally's apartment, he went in search of a store open on Christmas Day. He finally found a drug store that had a small toy section and picked out a dinosaur coloring book and some crayons. He had ten dollars on him—just enough for the toys and a gift bag to put them in. The cashier rang up his purchases and handed him his change—forty-five cents. That would have to hold him over until his unemployment check arrived, but Benny wasn't concerned. Christmas was all about giving, and the children at the shelter had even less than he had. He remembered the delight on Gabe's face over receiving something as simple as a coloring book and candy cane. That's what Christmas was all about. Besides, he had a good feeling about his future. If his interview at Sun Valley Country Club went well, there may be a steady income in his future. Pocketing the coins, Benny wished the cashier a Merry Christmas and headed for Hyatt House.

When he told the receptionist he had a gift for one of the children, she directed him to the common room. He walked through halls painted a soft, sky blue—soothing and light. At least the common room had splashes of cheery primary colors to liven it up. He peeked in the doorway and noticed Laura sitting on the floor. She was reading to about a dozen children of various ages who surrounded her. Gabe was tucked against one side of her, and a girl of about ten leaned on the other side.

Neither Laura nor the children noticed him in the doorway, so he listened while studying her, the way the light from the window turned her hair into shades of red and gold, the soft lilt of her voice as she read to the children, and how at home she looked sitting on the floor with her legs curled beneath her.

It wasn't until she reached the end of the story that Gabe glanced up and spotted him. "Mr. Benny!" he shouted, jumping to his feet and rushing across the room. "Did the magic box work? Did you get your wish?"

"Well," Benny said. "I got a fruitcake."

"You wished for a fruitcake?" Gabe's face scrunched up in a frown. "That's a dumb wish."

"I didn't exactly wish for a fruitcake. It just arrived."

Gabe shook his head. "Grownups."

Benny handed the gift bag to Gabe, who jumped up and down with excitement on seeing the dinosaur book. "Is this for me?"

"Sure is." Benny reached into the bag. "And this," he said, holding up a box of animal crackers, "is for you to share with your friends."

Gabe's eyes twinkled with delight. "Thank you, Mr. Benny Penny. You're the best." With that he took the box of animal crackers and scurried off to share them with his friends.

Laura then joined Benny, a half smile on her face. "That was nice," she said, then tilted her head. "Did I hear you say something about fruitcake?"

Benny nodded.

"It wasn't from Beverley's Bake Shop, was it?"

"Why yes, it was. Magical Fruitcake or some such thing."

"Sprinkled with pixie dust," Laura added.

"You know her?"

"I do. She also does some baking for the kids here at the shelter." An amused grin warmed her face. "She's Nick's wife."

"Mrs. Claus?"

This time Laura laughed out loud. "Don't let her hear you call her that."

"Does she at least wear a ruffled apron when she bakes?"

"Not hardly," Laura said with a shake of her head.

So, Nick's wife baked the fruitcake. The information only bolstered Benny's suspicion. "I figured Nick had something to do with this."

"Well, he must have taken a liking to you to go to all the trouble."

Benny didn't tell her about the book that was left on his doorstep as well. Maybe that was something they could talk about over coffee? He fingered the change in his pocket, realizing there wasn't enough left for coffee. He had his credit card, but he'd been keeping it under lock and key until his finances were back on track.

Laura brushed her hair away from her face and a diamond ring on her left hand sparkled in the light. An engagement ring. Damn, just his luck.

He would never hit on an engaged woman. He'd been the victim in a love triangle once before and knew from his past experience what it felt like to be cheated on. Unlike the man who'd destroyed his prior relationship, Benny had standards. Married and engaged women were off limits. Period.

Maybe it was better that Laura was involved with someone else. He had nothing to offer a woman. Not until he got back on his feet. If he was in a position to ask a woman out, however, someone like Laura would be at the top of his list. If he really did believe in magic, maybe a girl like her would be interested in a guy like him.

Before he could make an excuse to leave, Laura asked what his plans were for the day.

"Nothing much. My neighbor invited me over for Christmas dinner tonight."

"Don't you have family in town?"

Benny shook his head. "Nope, I just moved here a few months ago. My family is all over the place. We'll video chat tonight. If they can make time." He coughed to cover up the note of annoyance in his voice. "I mean, they're all busy and stuff. I understand."

She didn't say anything, just stared at him with a look that spoke volumes.

"What about you?" he asked. "Do you have family in town?"

Laura opened her mouth, then closed it. Her gaze shifted away and her face lost some of its animation. She looked back and shook her head. "No. No family in town."

The urge to ask her to join him was overpowering. But no. She had a fiancé to share Christmas with. He didn't have a fiancé or even a girlfriend, but he'd enjoy dinner with Mrs. Sobieski, then an evening of video conferencing with his family. It would be a very merry

Christmas, he told himself.

If nothing else, seeing the joy in Gabe's face when he ran across the room to thank him again for the book and crackers was the perfect start. He lowered himself to one knee and gave the boy a hug, promising to be back soon.

"Soon like in an hour?"

"No, but I'm sure you'll have lots of fun activities to keep you busy today."

Gabe chewed on his bottom lip, then asked in a hesitant voice. "Soon like tomorrow?"

Benny noticed Laura's gaze moving from him to the boy and back again as she followed the conversation.

"Yes, I can come by tomorrow."

Gabe clapped his hands together. "That's a promise, right?"

"Right." Benny wondered how many times promises had been broken in the boy's short life. "It's a promise you can count on."

Gabe wrapped his arms around Benny's neck, "Okay. And you don't even have to bring me another present."

Laura lowered her voice. "Gabe?"

Gabe's face was all innocence when he looked up at Laura. "I said he didn't have to."

Benny chuckled. "What if I want to."

Gabe turned back to Benny and turned his hands palm up. "Well, if you want to, it's okay. Right Miss Laura?"

Laura gave an indulgent shake of her head and smiled, then turned to Benny. "Don't get his hopes up," she said, the furrowed brow in sharp contrast to the smile on her face.

Benny had the impression she was talking about more than a simple gift. "I won't," he replied, more to erase the look of concern on her face than anything else.

He patted Gabe's head, then stood. "So, I guess I'll see you both tomorrow."

Laura shook her head. "Oh, I won't be here. I have to work tomorrow."

"I thought…" Benny shook his head. "Don't you work here?"

She laughed. "No, I just volunteer on my days off work."

Work where? he wanted to ask, but before he could form the question, Laura scurried off, gathering up the children for another story. He watched her go with a sense of lost opportunity, then remembered the ring on her finger and turned to leave.

He'd still keep his promise to Gabe, but a little of the sparkle had rubbed off of his promised visit.

****

If there was a way to define dinner at his neighbor's, Benny could only describe it as *interesting*. Sally had made Cornish game hens, which he found challenging, to say the least. The table was covered with condiment dishes filled with cranberry sauce, apple chutney, and brown gravy. It was hard to decide what went where. In addition, there were side dishes to consider, from corn to carrots and sweet potatoes covered with toasted pecans and marshmallows.

"How many people are you expecting?" Benny asked with a grin.

Sally gave him a gentle slap with a dish towel.

"Don't tease. I still think I'm cooking for six."

"You had four kids?" Ah, another something he didn't know about his neighbor. Up until now they'd had a casual *waving in the hallway* kind of relationship.

"Four of the best and brightest children you'll ever meet. Each one more successful than the last." She gazed off into the distance, a wistful smile on her face. "And they've blessed me with six grandchildren." She held up a finger. "Wait."

She hurried into the living room and came back with a frame containing six pictures. "This is Caelyn and Liam," she said. "Sarah's two." She pointed to the next pictures. "Tiffany's boys, Everett and Jace." Then the next. "Cadence and Harmony are the oldest. Michael's two girls."

Benny didn't want to ask the obvious question but couldn't help himself. "Why aren't they here?" *Helping us eat this mountain of food.*

Sally didn't seem to take offense. "Oh, they will be. It's a tradition passed down from my mother and grandmother. Each family spends Christmas day with their spouse and children. Then the following weekend we all come together for a big family celebration. It saves everyone from having to figure out whose house to go to and takes some of the stress out of the holidays."

Benny nodded. Seemed like a good enough reason, although if he had the chance, he'd spend every holiday with his family. Maybe, if things didn't work out, he'd move closer to one of his siblings, or move to Florida to be closer to his parents. Although they seemed to be getting along just fine without him.

Sally spooned more sweet potatoes onto his plate.

"What you don't finish you'll have to take home," she said. "I can't eat them with my diabetes."

"You could if they weren't smothered in brown sugar and marshmallows."

She gave a girlish grin. "What's the fun in that?"

Before he could respond, she snapped her fingers. "Oh, I forgot to tell you. Remember my friend Judy?"

He nodded.

"Well, she talked to her nephew and you have an interview scheduled for next week. Here, let me…" she scurried to the counter, moving aside papers and magazines until she found what she was looking for. She held up a slip of notepaper. "Here it is. You have an interview on Thursday at two o'clock with Jack Archer." She raised her eyes from the note. "That's Judy's nephew."

Benny reached for the paper. "I can't thank you enough," he said, truly touched that she'd gone out of her way for him. "And thank Judy as well."

"I will," she said. "I have a good feeling about this." She turned to the refrigerator. "Now for dessert."

****

Later that evening, after leaving Sally's apartment with a full belly and an armload of leftovers in plastic containers, Benny turned on his laptop. His family had scheduled a Christmas evening video chat since everyone would be busy during the day. Everyone but him.

He waited for the others to log on. Ten minutes went by and he wondered if he had the wrong time. Maybe they'd forgotten him. He was just getting ready to send out a text message when his computer chat chimed.

He saw part of his mother's chin. "Is this thing on? Benny, can you hear me?"

"I'm here, Mom."

The video shifted and her face came into focus. "There you are. Merry Christmas. Your dad's right here."

His father shifted into view, half in and half out of the picture. "Merry Christmas, son."

"How are you doing, dear?" his mother asked. "Any luck on the job front?"

"Not yet," he admitted. "But I…"

"I'm sure something will turn up soon," his mother said.

His father harrumphed, and Benny could feel the disappointment radiating through his computer screen. In a family of doctors and lawyers, Benny felt like the black sheep. Losing his job didn't help.

"Do you need anything?" his mother asked.

"No. Not at all." The last thing he was going to do was borrow money from his family. If he had to take a part-time job with a ride-share company or wash dishes at some greasy spoon, he would. But he wouldn't rely on his family to get him through.

Something would come along. He was sure of it. He pulled the notepaper out of his pocket. He didn't want to put all his hopes into one interview, but maybe the job at Sun Valley Country Club really was the answer to his wish.

At another chime, he glanced back at the screen. "There you are," he said seeing his brother Joe and his wife Kim.

"Sorry we're late. We took the girls to a movie and decided to stop for pizza afterward."

"That's okay, Mom and Dad just got here."

The girls clamored around the video screen. "Hi Uncle Benny. Can we open our presents yet?"

"Sure, go ahead." They'd decided a while back not to exchange gifts with each other since they were scattered all over the place, but to only send gifts to the kids.

The girls ripped open their boxes and exclaimed over the mermaid dolls and board games. "Thanks Uncle Benny. We love them!"

"Merry Christmas," he said. He'd dipped into his savings to buy Christmas gifts, skimping on groceries instead. It was a choice he'd make again, even if it meant eating a free dinner at the community center. Seeing the girls faces light up was worth it. "What did Santa bring you for Christmas?"

The girls talked over each other, using sheer volume to list all the gifts they'd received from Santa. While they opened their presents from his mother and father, Benny's sister came on the screen. She wore a black sheath dress set off by a sparkling necklace. Her husband wore a black suit with a red tie.

"Sorry we're late," Missy said, reaching up to put earrings on. "We're getting ready to meet with a few close friends from Tom's company. She urged their son Timmy forward. "Say hi to your Uncle Ben."

Timmy smiled. "Hi Uncle Ben."

Something about that gap-toothed grin reminded Benny of Gabe, which in turn made him think of Laura. He wondered how Gabe was spending his Christmas. He assumed Laura was with her fiancé, probably having a romantic dinner and exchanging gifts. The thought sent a wave of disappointment over him.

Keeping a smile plastered on his face grew more difficult. Forcing the smile, Benny focused his attention on to the video screen and his nephew. "Hi Timmy. How's my boy?"

Timmy's eyes glanced downward. His voice was soft and shy. "Good Uncle Benny."

Benny was surprised Timmy even remembered him. He probably wouldn't have said anything at all without his mother's urging. Missy's husband leaned into the screen with a grin. "Hey Ben," he said. "How're things working out?"

"Good," Benny replied. "I have a lead on a new job that may be perfect for me." It wasn't exactly a lie, but there was no need to bring everyone down on Christmas day.

"That's great," Tom said. He leaned forward and kissed the top of Missy's head. Benny heard him whisper, "The babysitter's here, hon."

Missy nodded, then turned to her son. "Look what your Uncle Ben got you," she exclaimed, opening the package Benny had sent. "The Lego set you've been wanting. Say thank you."

Timmy gave him that shy smile again. "Thank you, Uncle Benny."

"You're welcome." Benny was grateful Missy had given him a list of things her son would like, since Benny wasn't there in person to find out. He spent more time at the shelter than he did with his own nieces and nephews. That would change soon, however. Once he was gainfully employed again, he'd make it a point to fly out for regular visits.

"I'm sorry guys," Missy said. "We have to go, or we'll be late. Merry Christmas everyone! Say hi to

Diane when she gets here."

Mike laughed. "I don't think Diane has figured out the time difference yet." Since moving clear across the country, Diane was always getting mixed up about the time for phone calls and video chats.

"Why don't I just give her a call," Benny's mother said. "I'm sure she'd hate to miss seeing everyone."

"I just sent her a text," Joe said, efficient as always. Joe was the oldest and ready to take charge of any given situation.

Minutes later, Diane popped in. "Sorry guys. I haven't adjusted to the time difference yet."

"See? I told you," Joe said with a chuckle.

"Where's Missy?" Lauren asked. "Don't tell me I beat her here?"

"She's come and gone," Benny's mother said. "They had a Christmas party to attend, but she said to say hello. How are you feeling, dear?"

Diane glowed. "Good now that the morning sickness is over."

Greg's wife Cara chimed in with her pregnancy advice. Benny had the feeling he could just slip away, and no one would even notice.

The video chat was shorter than he would have liked and left him feeling empty and hollow inside. His siblings were anxious to get on with their own lives. Even his parents had plans to celebrate with friends for the evening. They were going out to dinner.

Everyone was distracted, apparently ready to get back to their own routine. As much as he missed them all, the raucous mayhem made him feel even more alone.

He glanced down at the note Sally had given him,

then back to the supposedly magic Christmas box on his counter and the notebook that had been left on his doorstep the next morning. Just a coincidence. He didn't want to get his hopes up, but couldn't help feeling as if something magical was about to happen,

Chapter Four

Later that week, Benny splurged on a haircut, gave himself a close shave and starched his shirt until it could have stood up without him.

Twenty minutes early for his interview, Benny paced outside the country club. This felt right. He gazed at the grounds, still covered with a few inches of snow. Come spring the grass would be lush. He imagined guests enjoying the grounds, swimming in the pool, and playing golf on the greens. This was something he wanted to be a part of. It felt as if he'd come home.

Benny was enthusiastic and felt an instant connection with Judy's nephew, Jack Archer, a man about his own age. The interview went well.

"One thing," Jack said. "You told me why this job would be perfect for you. What you didn't tell me is why *you're* the man for this job."

Benny was stumped for a moment. He'd put so much energy into finding the job best suited for him that he hadn't given much thought to his own qualifications and lack of experience. Then he remembered the notebook, and all of the reasons he was ideally suited for such a job.

He listed each one, then ended with a promise. "I would give one-hundred percent to this job," he said, with all honesty. "I'm dependable and this job is ideally suited to my strengths. I'll look forward to coming to work each morning and leave with a sense of satisfaction in a job well done each night."

Jack nodded and, with a handshake, brought the interview to a close. "I'll be in touch," he said.

That was over a week ago. Benny tried to hold out hope, but as the days went by, that hope dwindled like the last sputtering flame of a dying candle. When the phone finally rang, he was already expecting the worst.

"Benny, this is Jack Archer from Sun Valley Country Club. It's about the job you interviewed for. I'm sorry to say we went with one of the other applicants who was more qualified for this particular job. I wanted to tell you personally."

"I understand." Benny tried to hide the disappointment in his voice. "I hope you'll keep my resume on file if something else opens up."

"I will. If I hear about anything, I'll let you know," Jack said. "Good luck, Benny."

"Thanks, I would appreciate it," Benny thanked him and hung up. He'd been sure this was the right job for him. He drummed his fingers on the desk. He had two choices—either admit defeat and give up, or push on, assured that the right job was out there waiting for him.

****

He pulled up another job-search website and scrolled down, hoping to find something he was qualified for, but unless he became a nail technician or earned an overnight nursing degree, he'd already eliminated all viable options.

His job search was interrupted by a light triple tap on the door, Sally Sobieski's signature knock. "Come on in," he called. "It's unlocked." He specifically left it unlocked for her in the morning, but she refused to walk in without knocking first. She didn't have to worry about interrupting anything. It wasn't as if he was in a relationship or anything.

She came inside and dropped a package of English Muffins on the table. "They were buy one, get one free at the market," she said. "This is the free one."

He smiled. They'd formed a friendly bond over the last few weeks. She'd taken him under her wing, baking for him and making sure he ate. In return he would do odd jobs for her that required someone stronger or taller, which wasn't a difficult feat considering she barely came up to his chin.

Sally glanced at the computer. "I heard the bad news," she said. "If it's any comfort, Judy said her nephew really liked you, but this other guy had experience over at River's Bend Resorts and, you know…"

He nodded. "Understood. Jack was really nice. He said he'd keep me in mind."

She patted his shoulder. "You'll find something soon. I can feel it in my bones."

"That's just your bursitis."

She laughed. "You're probably right."

"Wait a minute." An idea suddenly popped into Benny's head. "This guy who was hired. If he worked at River's Bend, then they might be trying to fill his position. They probably just haven't gotten around to placing an ad in the paper yet."

Sally nodded. "That makes sense."

"I could go over there and get a jump on the competition."

"I think that's a great idea. But you should eat something first. You need to keep up your strength. All that talking…"

"Well, I just happen to have a package of the finest English Muffins here. Would you care to join me?"

She did and threw in a jar of her home-made peach preserves as well.

****

The next morning Benny copied his resume, put on his best interview clothes, and headed to River's Bend Resorts. He stopped at the front desk where a receptionist greeted him with a smile.

"How can I help you?"

"Hi, I'm here about the job opening?"

Her smile slipped a notch. "What job opening?"

"Well, I'm assuming there's an opening since one of your employees was recently hired by Sun Valley Country Club. I assumed you'd be hiring someone to fill his place, and I…well you know what they say? The early bird catches the worm."

She smiled again, but this time Benny could see it was forced. "Can you tell me the name of the employee?"

Benny began to feel uncomfortable. There was something wrong here. He pulled the slip of paper from his pocket where Sally had written the name of the person who'd taken the position at Sun Valley Country Club. "Roger," he said. "Roger Fletcher."

Her expression hardened. "One moment." She pressed a button on the intercom system. "Mr. Ellis, there's someone here to see you about Roger Fletcher." She listened and nodded her head, then turned to Benny. "Mr. Ellis will see you. You can go right in."

The office manager stood when Benny entered his office. He scowled. "If Roger Fletcher sent you here for a recommendation, he can forget it. I was hoping I'd seen the last of that no-good bum."

Benny was taken aback by the man's attitude. "No," he stammered. "I was under the impression he left here on good terms, leaving an opening on your staff."

"That opening was filled six months ago when I fired Fletcher."

Benny blinked away his confusion. "Six months ago?"

The office manager cocked his head. "Did he tell you I'd give him a reference? If so, he's sadly mistaken."

"I, um…no. I'm sorry I wasted your time." Benny didn't ask why the man was fired. What good would that do?

And so, it was back to the drawing board for Benny. He had to tell Sally something when she asked how it went, so he simply said the man had left his position several weeks ago and the job had already been filled. It wouldn't do him any good to ruin another man's life. Besides, it was only one side of the story. Everyone deserved a second chance.

Luckily his unemployment check arrived in the afternoon mail, so he had some breathing space. That and a few temporary jobs would keep him afloat until the right position came along.

****

The smell of freshly-ground coffee greeted Laura when she entered the bookstore. Ivy waved from behind the counter. The barista wore a turquoise apron, which matched the turquoise streak in her snow-white hair. Ivy was a born-again hippie, working part-time at Laura's shop to supplement her social security check. She was efficient, hard-working, and quick with a smile or a joke for the customers. Laura wasn't sure how she ever survived without her.

"What's our special of the day?" Ivy asked.

"Old-Fashioned Gingerbread Cake." Laura set her covered containers on the counter.

Ivy lifted the lid and the aroma of molasses and cloves wafted up. "Mmmm…still warm."

Laura nodded. Aside from books, cooking was her passion. She loved trying new recipes, and it was her idea to have a single "Dessert of the Day" at the coffee counter. So far no one had complained, and there were rarely any leftovers to bring home. It was simply one of the ways she adjusted her business plan to meet a changing market where book sales had declined considerably.

"I made extra," Laura said. "We have the writer's group meeting here today, and they usually break at ten for coffee and a snack."

"Discount?"

"Ten percent, as usual."

Ivy shook her head. "It's a wonder you're able to stay in business at all."

Laura simply smiled. She had a good working relationship with the local writers, running sales and events at her shop, as well as having group author signings twice a year. "It's a two-way street," she said. "Bookstores need authors and authors need to sell their books."

"But you give away more books than you sell."

This was a conversation they'd had before, but it never failed to reinforce Laura's beliefs. "It isn't about selling books to make a profit," she said. "It's about making books accessible for people." To that end, she'd added audio books and ebooks to the mix, which customers could listen to for free as long as they were in the store.

"That's why I call it The Reading Room, rather than just another bookstore. It's about opening new worlds for children and adults, giving them a place to escape." What she didn't say was that was exactly what books were to her as a child...a means of escape. Maybe that was why opening a bookstore had been a dream from the time she was young enough to lose herself in books. The bookstore had turned into a bookstore/lending library/coffee shop, but the dream was the same. She'd simply had to adapt it to a changing market.

She could still hear Edna's voice in her head. "Never give up on your dreams," she'd said. Laura hadn't then, and she wouldn't now. She'd find new and innovative ways to keep the store open.

Ivy and Laura both glanced up at a knock at the door. Two eyes, framed with bushy gray eyebrows, peered directly over the CLOSED sign.

Laura shook her head and smiled. "Guess we're opening a little early," she said.

Ivy slid a cup onto the counter. "I'm ready if you are."

Laura unlocked the door, flipped the sign to OPEN and ushered in Lou Burton, a morning regular. He tipped an imaginary cap. "Morning, Miss Laura," he said, then turned and winked at Ivy. "And how are you this fine morning, pretty lady."

Ivy actually blushed and turned to pour Lou's coffee, then placed it on the counter. "Right as rain," she replied.

"Righter than rain from where I'm sitting." He glanced at the pastry container. "What marvelous delight do we have here today?"

"Gingerbread cake," Laura answered, joining them at the counter. "Do you like gingerbread?"

Lou patted his stomach. "I never met a dessert I didn't like."

Laura cut him a slice. "This one's on the house," she said, ignoring Ivy's look of disapproval. What was a piece of cake compared to customer loyalty? Besides, she knew Lou would make up for it by leaving Ivy a generous tip.

Laura left the coffee counter to set up the meeting room for the writers' group. She arranged the tables and set out pitchers of ice water. She loved having the group at her store. As someone who loved to read, writers were the magicians who created the worlds and events where she could escape. The published authors were always willing to show up for readings and book signings, both of which were popular in their community. Not to mention the writers were some of her best customers as well.

A symbiotic relationship—that's what it was. Readers needed authors and authors needed readers. And no one needed writers as much as Laura. She went through two or three books a week—mysteries, romances, thrillers, and biographies. She loved them all.

Laura was setting up the overhead projector when

some of the writers began showing up. They came in all ages, shapes, and sizes, but to Laura they were magical, every one of them. "Can I get you anything else?"

Jocelyn, the current president of the group, shook her head. "No, thanks. We're good to go."

Still Laura lingered. "What's your meeting about today?"

"Formatting manuscripts for publication."

Laura nodded. More and more of her authors were independently published. She had a special section for Indies. Most of them went out of their way to promote and market their work locally, which was great for bringing traffic into the store. Laura had no genre preferences, and stories were stories, whether in print, electronic format, or audio.

For a moment Laura was tempted to ask if she could sit in on the workshop. Not that she had any desire to write. She simply enjoyed being surrounded by writers, absorbing their creativity, and getting a glimpse inside their imaginations. She expected if it was visible, the room would sparkle with it, and the air grow dense with the weight of ideas. At least that's the way the meeting day felt to her.

Laura left as more people filed in, taking seats, and spreading notebooks and laptops on the table. At the coffee counter, Ivy chatted with an older woman with graying hair and wearing a pumpkin colored pantsuit. Ivy introduced Laura to her friend Sally Sobieski.

"Nice to meet you, Sally."

"Thank you," she said, clutching a notebook to her chest. "Ivy told me about the writers' group that meets here, and I thought I'd give it a try."

"It's open to the public. I'm not in charge, but I'd

be happy to introduce you to the president of the group."

"Oh." Sally gripped her notebook tighter, eyes darting left and right. "Maybe. I'm not sure I'm ready."

Laura gave her arm a gentle pat. "You'll never know until you try. I can promise you they're a lovely group of people. What are you working on?"

"I've been working on my memoirs for years. Ivy has convinced me to consider submitting them for publication, but I'm not sure where to start. She told me that the writers' group would be able to help."

Lou Burton leaned close. "I'd love to hear about your adventures. Perhaps over dinner?"

Ivy laughed and leaned toward Sally. "Don't mind Lou. He flirts with everyone."

Sally gave him a bright smile. "I'd love to join you for dinner. But I have to warn you, I'm not a cheap date."

Lou looked surprised, as if he hadn't expected her to take him seriously. "Well," he said. "Let's set a date and time."

Sally opened her notebook and wrote down her phone number, then tore the sheet off and handed it to Lou. "Call me," she said.

Lou tucked the piece of paper into his wallet. "I will," he assured her with a nod.

Sally turned to Laura. "Ivy gave me one of your newsletters. I hope you include the recipe for the gingerbread cake in the next one. This is delicious!"

"I'll do just that. It seems to already be a popular choice. Swing by the register later and sign up for the newsletter so you'll receive it every month."

"Thanks." Sally took a deep breath and

straightened her spine. "It's now or never," she said with a grin, then turned to enter the workshop room. "Wish me luck," she called over her shoulder.

Laura, Ivy, and Lou wished her luck in unison.

"She seems like a sweet lady," Laura observed.

"She is. And she's had an incredible past. I've been telling her to get those memoirs finished for years. Do you know she was Miss Alabama 1962? And she joined the circus for a few years, raised a family, and was the first woman to run for office on the Town Council."

"What? Wow." Laura watched Sally hesitate at the door to the meeting room, then she straightened her back and lifted her shoulders before walking inside. "Who'd have known? I guess everyone has a story," she said.

And that gave her a great idea. She was looking for more content to add to her newsletter, which included a recipe of the month as well as a column called *Laura's Likes*. Her column reviewed books that had been newly released that month.

She turned to Ivy. "What would you think about adding a new column to the newsletter? Something like…" she thought out loud. "People you should know, or…"

"Don't judge a book by its cover," Lou suggested, staring at the space where Sally had disappeared into the meeting room.

Laura clapped. "Perfect! And I think I'll ask Sally to be one of my first guests."

Chapter Five

It was a Wednesday afternoon in February. Sunlight eased the winter chill from the air, hinting at warmer weather to come. Benny had just returned from another round of job interviews when the phone rang.

"Oh Benny," Mrs. Sobieski said. "I was hoping you were home. Could I bother you for a favor?"

"Of course," he said. "What can I do for you?"

"Well, I'm here at the Country Club with Judy having lunch. Wednesdays they have a lovely crab cake special. Have you tried it?"

"No," he said with an indulgent smile. "I'm afraid not."

"Well, you simply must. The chef here is from Maryland and makes authentic Maryland crab cakes with Old Bay seasoning. I tell you, they're to die for."

Benny let his neighbor ramble on, knowing she'd get to the point eventually.

"So anyway," she said. "When I went to start my car after lunch it wouldn't start at all. Nothing. I can't imagine what's wrong with it. I just filled the gas tank, so that's not it. Maybe the battery?"

"Could be," Benny said. "Why don't I come out there and take a look at it for you? If it's something I can't fix, then I'll bring you girls home and send a mechanic to check it out."

"Oh, you're a love," she said. "I knew I could count on you."

It only took Benny fifteen minutes to get to the Country Club. While driving toward the entrance, a feeling of déjà vu washed over him. He couldn't shake the conviction that this was where he was meant to work. He liked the look of the place—liked the idea of spending his days on the sunlit grounds or inside where the burnished wood counters, subtly patterned wallpaper, and layered textures screamed casual elegance.

He walked through the lobby to the screened patio, admiring again the white-washed stone deck dotted with wrought iron tables and royal blue umbrella shades. Sunlight, coupled with patio heaters, warded off the chill. Sally and her friend Judy sat at a table laughing over cocktails, along with Judy's nephew Jack Archer.

Jack stood, shook his hand, and greeted him, "Benny, what a coincidence."

Before Benny could ask why, Judy spoke up, "Jack, didn't Benny interview for the same job as that person you just fired?"

Benny spun around to face Judy. "Fired?"

Sally spoke up. "Can you imagine? He showed up for work drunk this morning. Who drinks that early in the morning?"

Benny glanced at Sally's drink with a raised eyebrow.

She placed her hand over her glass. "This is a *virgin* strawberry daiquiri," she said. "And I'm not working."

"That wasn't the first time he was caught drinking

on the job, either," Judy interjected. "Jack is fair, but three times and you're out." She turned to her nephew. "Isn't that right, Jackie?"

The man nodded. "My aunt is right about one thing, Benny. You were at the top of my list before, and if you're interested in the job, come see me in the morning to fill out some paperwork. You can start as soon as possible.

"I could start today," Benny said eagerly.

Jack smiled. "Monday will be fine." He reached out and shook Benny's hand. "And I appreciate you starting on such short notice."

"You won't be sorry," Sally interjected. "Benny's a hard worker and doesn't drink hardly at all, let alone during working hours."

Jack chuckled. "Thanks for the recommendation." He turned to Benny. "What a lucky coincidence that you happened to come by today."

"Yes," Benny said in agreement. "I guess it's a good thing Mrs. Sobieski's car didn't start." He glanced over at his neighbor just in time to see a guilty look pass between Sally and Judy. Suddenly, it all made sense. They'd engineered the entire meeting.

Sally blinked. "You know," she said. "Sometimes if I don't put my gas cap on tight enough the car doesn't start. I wonder if that's what happened?"

"Could be," Benny said with a smile. "I'll check that first thing." He couldn't be mad at her for engineering this whole meeting, especially considering how it had all turned out.

****

And so it was, through a series of fortunate connections, that Benny started working at Sun Valley

Golf Course and Country Club.

With his first paycheck, he took Sally and her friend Judy to dinner at an Italian restaurant. The three of them toasted his good fortune with a bottle of red wine.

Sally lifted her glass. "To continued success in your new job."

"Thank you," Benny said, clinking glasses. "Thank you both."

"Don't forget the magic box," Sally said.

Judy perked up. "Magic box? Do tell!"

Benny shook his head and raised his eyes skyward. "It's nothing, just someone's idea of a joke."

"Santa Claus gave it to him," Sally explained. "He gets to make three wishes. His first wish was for a job and look what happened. It's a miracle!"

Benny almost regretted having told Sally about the box. It seemed like that was all she could talk about these days.

"Getting the job wasn't a miracle, and there's no such thing as magic," he assured them. "If it hadn't been for you two, I'd still be scouring the help wanted ads for a job."

"But it's still pretty amazing. You made a wish, and the next morning you got a journal to find out what your perfect job would be. And a fruitcake."

"I love fruitcake," Judy said, buttering a roll. "Was it from Beverley's Bake Shop? Her Magic Fruitcake with pixie dust sprinkles is the bomb?"

"The bomb?"

Judy nodded. "Isn't that what you young kids say?"

Before he could respond, Sally jumped in. "That's the one, all right. Beverley's Magic Fruitcake."

Judy turned back to Bennie. "That's the best. It's famous around here." She tilted her head. "Did you say there was a journal as well? What was in the journal?"

"Some questions about what I'd look for in the perfect career. Things I could have figured out for myself if I'd tried."

Sally pointed a breadstick at Benny. "You wouldn't have thought of those things without the journal, and you wouldn't have even mentioned looking for a different kind of job if you hadn't brought over a piece of that fruitcake. See? Magic box and magic fruitcake. It's all connected."

"I guess so," Benny relented. Sally was right about one thing. Just as she'd predicted, he looked forward to going to work every morning, something that wouldn't have happened if he hadn't answered the questions about what kind of job would suit him best. However, he didn't believe the box *or* the fruitcake were magic. A combination of all three items working together had made the magic happen.

"What are you going to wish for now?" Judy asked.

Benny shrugged. "I haven't thought about it." But now that she mentioned it, he remembered Nick saying he couldn't make his second wish until the first one had come true. If that was the case, now was the time to start thinking of another wish. Assuming he believed in magic, that is.

Judy pursed her lips. "I wonder what I'd wish for if I had a magic box."

Sally piped up. "I'd wish for a house. A big house with a swimming pool. And a privacy fence so I could skinny dip in my pool."

Judy groaned and covered her eyes. "I don't even want to see *myself* naked."

"Hmmm…maybe an indoor pool," Sally said.

Benny covered his ears and laughed. He'd thought about wishing for a house, but he didn't need to wish for one. With a stable income came the ability to buy a house on his own. *No magic necessary.*

Besides, even though he'd thought the first thing he'd do once he had a job was get a new place to live, he was concerned about leaving Sally alone at the apartment building. They'd grown accustomed to each other's company, and though she would never impose, she depended on him to be there if she needed him.

Sally tapped her chin. "Maybe I'd wish for a new car. One of those cute little Mini Coopers or something. A convertible I think."

Benny gave her a quick hug. "Just be sure to keep the gas cap on tight."

Sally's eyes opened wide in feigned innocence before they all had a good laugh. Benny gave her an encouraging smile to let her know how much he appreciated her ruse to get him in the right place at the right time. "Thank you," he mouthed.

Just then the servers arrived with their dishes and there was no more talk about wishes or magic Christmas boxes.

****

Across town, Laura frowned over her account sheets. Her security slipped away with each passing month. Profits steadily dropped despite her attempts to find new and innovative ways to bring in customers. The bank account dwindled, frightening her, and she discovered the downswing in the economy wasn't singularly affecting her store. Small business owners everywhere struggled to stay out of the red. Even some of the bigger chains were having problems keeping afloat.

She poured a glass of wine and printed out a spread sheet. If things kept going the way they were, she'd be filing for bankruptcy in less than three years. Unless she came up with some new way to make money.

Too bad she didn't have Nick's magic box.

She sipped on her wine and let the thought percolate. That wasn't such a bad idea. Not the magic part, but the box. A mystery box. Hmmm…

She could fill it with a book, bookmark, maybe a gift card and something that symbolically represented the theme of the book. Wrap them up and put a ribbon on top and sell the boxes as last-minute surprise gifts.

She grabbed a pencil and paper and began making notes of some of her favorite books and what she could include in a package with them. By the time she was done, she'd filled three pages, along with ideas for a display table with wrapped gift boxes, helium balloons, and a banner reading SURPRISE!

Excitement had her scribbling furiously as one idea followed another. She could create a variety of mystery boxes for children and boxes for different holidays. Some boxes could have surprises inside that corresponded to certain pages in the book.

Mulling over her notes and sketches, Laura smiled. She took the wine glass into the kitchen and washed, dried, and put it away while contemplating how Benny's magic box had inspired an idea that could be the answer to her worries. Tonight, she'd rest without the anxiety that had been eating at her these last few months.

****

The next morning, Laura bounded through the bookstore's front door earlier than usual, eager to share her plans with Ivy. Drinking a cup of the house special, she laid out each page and described her ideas, then released a sigh. "What do you think?"

"Wow." Ivy glanced from one page to the next. "I think it's brilliant!" She ran a finger down Laura's list of items to include in the boxes and added a few of her own. "How about pens, key chains, and candles? And ornaments for the Christmas boxes."

"Yes." Ivy's excitement was contagious. Laura scribbled their ideas on a separate piece of paper, then tapped the pencil against her lips. "I bet some of the authors in the writer's group would be happy to put together a package of their own books every once in awhile."

"I'm sure they would." Ivy agreed. "It would be a great promotion for them, too."

Laura figured there'd be a few kinks to work out, but the idea had merit and with a little more brainstorming, they'd have a solid program ready to roll out over the next few months.

She envisioned the profit line on her spreadsheet rising as the possibility of bankruptcy faded. She felt something inside her unwind, something that had been wrapped in coils of fear and doubt. She took a deep breath and relaxed, really relaxed, for the first time in weeks.

Chapter Six

Easter came early that year. Benny thought about visiting the shelter, but Carol said they had special plans for the day. He missed Gabe. And, truth be told, he missed running into Laura. Just thinking about her brought a smile to his face—the way her eyes gave away her mood even before she spoke, the way her voice turned up at the end of a sentence, inviting him to respond.

He wished…no, he would never wish unhappiness on someone else, even if it meant he'd be free to pursue her. If only she were single. Now that he had a steady income, he could do more than ask her out for coffee. He could splurge on a fancy restaurant, show her that he was no longer down on his luck, but putting money in the bank and saving up for airline tickets to visit his family. He was hoping to have enough to surprise them next Christmas.

Sally had invited Benny over for Easter dinner. He'd offered to bring dessert, which was a good excuse to stop at Beverley's Bake Shop to pick something up. He probably should have stopped in sooner to tell Beverley how much he enjoyed her fruitcake, but hearing she was Nick's wife had thrown him for a loop. As soon as he opened the door to the bakery, the scents of fresh-baked breads, sugar, and cinnamon overwhelmed him. It smelled exactly like a bakery should smell.

Beverley, however, was the exact opposite of what he imagined Mrs. Claus would look like. She was tall and regal, with a black apron that set off the strand of pearls around her neck. Her hair was steel gray with a wide silver streak that seemed to glitter, as if dusted with pixie dust. Or probably sugar.

Benny didn't have to ask if she was the person he was looking for since her name was on her apron. He held out his hand and introduced himself with a little backstory about Christmas.

"Oh," she said. "You must be Nick's friend."

"I am," he replied. "I understand Nick is your husband. Have you been married long?"

Her smile held a hint of mystery. "Seems like forever. We met at the shelter years ago. I was the cook there. Nick donated eggs every weekend…"

"Eggs? Our Nick?"

"Yes, our Nick. When he's not playing Santa, he raises chickens and sells eggs."

Benny frowned. "Santa is an egg farmer?"

"No, Nick is an egg farmer who sometimes plays Santa Claus."

"Point taken."

"So," she continued. "Nick donated eggs on Saturdays, and I'd spend Sundays stretching them as far as I could. Eventually I turned my baking skills into a business."

"And a successful one from what I hear." Nick scanned the shelves of baked goods, each one more enticing than the one before. "Someone left me one of your fruitcakes for Christmas," he said. "It was delicious."

"Thank you."

"You wouldn't happen to know who sent it, would you?"

She shook her head. "I sell so many fruitcakes at Christmas, it would be impossible to say."

Benny hadn't expected her to come right out and claim it was Nick, so he changed the subject. "I'm looking for something to bring to a friend's house for Easter dinner. Do you have anything as magical as your fruitcake?"

"No, only the fruitcake has magical properties. But carrot cake is a good choice."

Nick smiled. "I get it. Easter bunnies and carrots, right?"

She tilted her head and pointed to the bakery rack. "Hot cross buns are also popular this time of year."

"No, I think I want something more special. A real showstopper." He frowned, remembering that Sally didn't eat sweets. "You wouldn't have anything sugar-free, would you?

Beverley held out her hand. "As a matter of fact, I do. Wait here," she said. "I might have just the thing you're looking for."

While Benny waited for her to return, he moved from one display case to the next, admiring the cakes, pies, and pastries.

Beverley returned with a cake unlike any he'd seen before. It was a layer cake, but the top was covered with something that looked like a bird's nest filled with multi-colored eggs and smaller speckled candy eggs around the outside.

Benny pointed to the nest. "Caramel?"

"Spun sugar," she replied. "But once you lift the nest off the top, the rest of the cake is low in sugar. I use applesauce to sweeten the cake, and a light whipped cream and unsweetened raspberries between the layers. Not only is it delicious, if I do say so myself, no one will ever suspect that it's actually healthy as well."

Benny knew this was the one. "I'll take it," he said. "My friend will love it."

"I'll box it up for you." She turned and placed the cake on the counter, then peeked over her shoulder. "Your friend wouldn't be Laura Lee Bell, would it?"

Her question took him by surprise. "No, why?"

When she turned with the boxed cake, her face was the model of innocence. "No reason. Just wondering."

Benny simply assumed she'd gotten him mixed up with someone else. She rang up the order with no further comments, but he couldn't help wondering about her question on his way home.

A few minutes later, when Laura showed up at the bakery to pick up her order of hot cross buns, Beverley said, "Oh, you missed your friend." She carefully placed Laura's boxed rolls on the counter.

"Friend?

"Benny. You know. Nick gave him the Christmas box."

"Oh, yes. That Benny. To be honest, I barely know him. We've run into each other from time to time, but that's it." Actually, the last time she'd seen Benny was weeks ago. They hadn't run into each other since, but that didn't stop her from watching for him. Watching and waiting. Which wasn't like her at all.

"I see." Beverley said, ringing up Laura's order. "Are you bringing these to Edna?"

Laura nodded and smiled. "You know she loves her sweets."

"She does. Nick and I stopped by to see her last week." Beverley let out a slow sigh. "She's worried about you. Made us promise to look out for you if anything happens to her."

"Oh." The thought of losing Edna tightened her chest. The ache was familiar. Why did everyone always leave her? It was almost as if she was meant to be alone forever. This was why she resisted emotional entanglements. Loving someone only left behind heartbreak when they were gone.

****

Edna had coffee brewing when Laura arrived. "Hot cross buns fresh from Beverley's Bake Shop," she announced, handing the box to Edna.

"That woman has magic fingers," Edna said, lifting the lid of the box and taking a deep whiff. "Mmmm…smells like heaven."

She started to rise, but Laura stopped her. "You stay there. I'll pour the coffee."

Edna pointed to the kitchen counter. "Use the Easter plates I pulled out. And the Easter napkins."

Laura took the hot cross buns back and set them on the counter, then poured two cups of coffee—black for her and sweet and light for Edna—and placed a hot cross bun on each plate. She set Edna's plate and cup on a serving tray, along with a fork and napkin, and placed it on the side table. "I hear Nick and Beverley were here last week."

Edna shook her head. "I still can't believe those two. Different as night and day. Who'd have thought they'd be a couple?"

Laura carried her own tray over and sat beside Edna. "Beverley said you were worried about me."

Edna reached out and took Laura's hand. "I do worry. I don't want you to be alone."

"There's nothing wrong with being alone."

Edna squeezed Laura's hand. "There's also nothing wrong with seeking out companionship. I'm not talking about a commitment, but someone to talk to, go out to dinner with, or to walk beside in the park."

Laura shook her head. "I don't need a companion. I have friends."

Edna tipped her head back and looked down her nose. "Beverley, Nick, and I? You need friends your own age."

Laura huffed. "I don't have time for friends. I'm busy with the bookstore."

"That's because all of your friends live inside books."

"That's not..." Laura couldn't even work up the energy to deny it. What Edna said was true. The characters in books were more real to her than anyone in her own life.

"I'm friends with Carol at the shelter," she said half-heartedly. It was mostly true. But if it would make Edna worry less, she'd try harder.

****

By the time summer rolled around, Benny had already received a raise and a promotion. Each day brought something different to do at the Country Club, and with the warmer weather more of his time was tied up handling jobs outside in the fresh air and sunshine. With the sun on his face and a soft breeze tousling his hair, he felt like the luckiest man on earth.

Benny was amazed how his life had turned around since Christmas. However, he still wasn't convinced that magic had anything to do with it. As the months went by, he'd started thinking about his next wish. He had a job he loved and extra money in his bank account, but it would be nice to have someone to share it with?

As soon as the thought registered, Laura's face came to mind. What was it about the woman that intrigued him so much? Was it because she was unavailable that he couldn't get her out of his mind? No, he realized, it was more than that. He didn't believe in soul mates or love at first sight. And yet, there was something about her that made him want to get to know her better. Some instinct told him that getting to know her on a deeper level, would lead to something far more serious.

He was getting ready to leave for the day when Sally called to invite him for dinner because she had something important to tell him.

"Can I bring anything?" he asked.

"Yes," she replied. "Bring champagne. We're celebrating."

Celebrating? Benny had an idea what that celebration might be. Sally had been diligently working on her memoirs for the last few months. He suspected she'd finally finished. Maybe she'd even let him read what she'd written. She hadn't wanted to share her manuscript while it was still in draft form.

The wine and beverage center was only a few blocks away, so Benny decided to walk. He passed by the shelter on his way and peeked inside the front window, hoping to catch sight of Laura. However, there was no sign of her. Just as well. She'd probably think he was a crazed stalker.

Champagne in hand, he turned back to the apartment and knocked on Sally's door. The rich scent of lasagna and warm bread fresh from the oven greeted him as he walked in the door. "You sure know the way to my heart," he teased.

Sally blushed. "If I was twenty years younger..."

Benny handed her the champagne to put on ice. He pulled up a chair at the table, noting it was set with her best china and a single red rose in a crystal vase. "What are we celebrating?"

Sally put her hands over her mouth but couldn't cover up the smile. "I published my book," she said in a breathless whisper.

Benny's jaw dropped. "What? How is that possible? I didn't even know you'd finished."

"Well, one of the gals at the writers' group helped me edit it and format the manuscript. Then I bought a cover online and uploaded it. Piece of cake."

"Seriously?" Benny was more than impressed. She certainly blew away the stereotype of a helpless Grandma who couldn't even turn on her computer. "Wow, congratulations. When can I read it?"

"Not until the release party next month."

She held out a piece of paper, and Benny studied it. There was a picture of Sally above the article.

DON'T JUDGE A BOOK BY ITS COVER

Sally Sobieski is living proof that it's never too late to follow your dreams. Her memoirs, titled Everything and the Kitchen Sink, explores the many varied and interesting career choices this grandmother of six has experienced, from beauty queen to circus clown to town council representative. Now she can add published author to her list of accomplishments.

Benny read the entire article while Sally brought the tray of lasagna from the kitchen and set it on the table.

Benny glanced at the other articles—*LAURA'S LIKES*, which reviewed several books, *FREE TO READ*, *RECIPE OF THE MONTH*, and *MEET THE AUTHOR*.

Then he saw the picture of Laura. She looked just like... He held the newsletter out to Sally. "Who's this?"

"Oh, that's Laura Lee Bell, the owner of the bookstore. My friend Ivy works there." Sally slid a square of lasagna onto Benny's dish as she chattered. "Ivy's real name is Evelyn, but she went all hippie punk on us and dyed a streak in her hair and insists we call her Ivy."

Benny smiled. "I don't think hippie punk is a word."

"Eat your lasagna before it gets cold," she said in mock reproach. "Anyway, my friend Ivy works at the bookstore and she told me they had a writers' group there. So, I went, and they were all so nice. That's when I seriously started working on getting my memoirs published."

"Just a few months ago?"

"Well, I didn't just start then. I'd been working on them for years, but it was a mess—papers and notes all over the place. With the help of the writers' group, I learned how to pull it all together, and now, *voila*!"

Benny shook his head. "*Voila*? You make it sound so simple."

"Well," she said. "Compared to some of the other

things I've done in my life, it was relatively simple."

"I can't wait to read it," Benny said. His thoughts, however, were drawn to the woman whose picture graced the newsletter. Who'd have thought Laura owned a bookstore? But tonight was about Sally and her achievements. He pushed thoughts of Laura from his mind and concentrated on Sally as she documented her journey to publication and all the people who'd helped her along the way.

Tomorrow, he promised himself. Tomorrow he'd drop by the bookstore and check out some books.

****

The next morning was a Saturday. Benny hadn't thought to ask Sally if the bookstore was open on the weekends. He assumed it would be but prepared himself for disappointment in case he was wrong.

He found the bookstore easy enough, but simply stood outside for a moment looking inside. A spring-themed window display in soft pastel shades showcased a variety of books, potted daisies and clusters of decorated Easter eggs. He stepped inside. First, he couldn't miss the scent of coffee beans, followed by a more subtle sandalwood, pine, and paper. Suddenly Benny was awash in all the small details that created the unique experience that was Laura's bookstore—the distinctions between this perfect hideaway and a big corporate store. The cozy reading nooks spaced throughout, local artists' paintings hung at eye level, the open space designed with book shelves angled along the outer walls, and displays scattered on antique tables…a store that begged customers to take a seat and make themselves at home.

On a circular table by the register he noticed a

curious display of wrapped gift boxes and wondered what they were all about. He made a mental note to ask Laura.

But she was nowhere to be found.

He ambled toward the coffee counter where a woman with a turquoise streak in her hair waited. "You must be Ivy," he said.

"I am. And you are?"

"Benny Carter. I'm a friend of Sally Sobieski."

The woman's face brightened. "Of course. She's talked about what a good neighbor you've been." Ivy placed an empty mug in front of him. "Cute," he said, reading the quote on the cup, *Happiness is a Cup of Coffee and a Good Book*. "On the house," Ivy said. "What's your poison?"

"I wouldn't open with that," Benny said with a smile. He glanced at the laminated list of specials—lattes and cappuccinos and macchiato. "I'll just have your regular brew."

"I have a nice fair-trade Sumatra blend today. I highly recommend it."

Benny made himself comfortable on the high stool. "Sounds perfect. Black, no sugar."

Ivy gave him a high five. "That's the best way to drink it, in my opinion." She turned to reach for a pot to fill his mug, then set it on the countertop in front of him.

Benny lifted the mug, blew across the surface and took a sip. "Mmmm...good choice. You do know your coffee beans."

Ivy preened at the compliment.

When Benny spoke again, he made an effort to keep his voice casual. "I was hoping to see the owner.

Laura, right? Is she here?"

"She's in the back room setting up for a class. Want me to get her?"

"No," Benny was quick to reply. "I plan on doing some shopping anyway. I'll talk to her when she's finished." He pointed to the gift box display and asked Ivy about it.

"Oh, that's a new idea Laura came up with. Mystery gift boxes filled with book-related items. Takes the pain out of buying a gift for someone."

Benny nodded. "That sounds like a great idea. I'll buy one for Sally's book launch party."

"Oh, if it's for Sally, then I'd suggest the navy blue one with gold stars. I helped pack that one myself, and it has a notebook and a fancy feathered pen inside, as well as a book about famous writers. I think Sally would love it." She winked. "I actually had her in mind when I filled it."

"Then that's the one I'll buy," Benny said. "Thanks for the suggestion."

After finishing his coffee, Benny wandered around the bookstore. He placed the blue gift package aside to buy, then decided to check out the children's section. He found a dinosaur book for Gabe, as well as an assortment of children's books to donate to the shelter.

Just then Laura walked by. Benny's breath caught in his throat. She was even prettier than he remembered. Her shoulder-length hair was pulled up into some sort of twirly bun, with a pencil holding it in place. Wispy strands framed her face and those smoky eyes glanced at him, then back in a double take. She stopped in her tracks and blinked. "Benny?"

He was ridiculously pleased. "You remembered

me…my name?"

Laura laughed. "Gabe and his Benny Penny. How could I forget?"

She immediately noticed the change in him. He looked more confident and at ease now, where before he had seemed beaten and lost. The first time she'd seen him he'd been eating a free meal at the community center. Today he was clean shaven and wearing a crisp linen shirt. Obviously, things had improved since that day.

She glanced at the stack of children's books in his arms. "You have kids?" She immediately regretted the question. It sounded as if she was digging for information about his personal life. Which she wasn't.

He smiled, seeming to take no offense at her question. "Just nieces and nephews," he said. "I'm their favorite uncle."

The smile brightened his face, like opening the curtains on a summer morning and letting the sunlight in. "Let me guess," she said. "Are you their only uncle?"

"You caught me," he said with a chuckle. "But that doesn't stop me from wearing the title with pride."

A family man, she thought. No wonder he'd been so good with Gabe. "Do you go to the shelter often?" she asked, reaching out and taking half the books from the pile in his arms.

"Thanks. I try to get over there once a week or so. Usually on weekends when I'm not working. Actually, I plan on taking some of these books to the shelter. I noticed the kids really enjoy reading."

He immediately climbed several notches in her estimation. "You're right. Sometimes reading is the only escape they have." He didn't have to know that she was speaking from experience.

They carried the books to the counter where the rest of his purchases awaited. Laura eyed the pile. "Do you mind if I ask you a question?"

He leaned against the counter, meeting her gaze. "Go ahead."

"Well," she cleared her throat, not sure how to address the issue. "Things seem to be going better for you since last I saw you."

He nodded. "Yes, things are going much better. I'd lost my job right before I met you last Christmas. Taylor and Grant Department Stores closed without warning."

"Oh, I remember hearing about that. Hundreds of people lost their jobs and benefits, right?"

"Yeah, I was one of them."

"I'm sorry to hear that. I thought…" She didn't want to tell him what she'd thought—that he was homeless and destitute by choice. She was ashamed of herself for making such a rash judgment. Ironic since her new column was about not judging a book by its cover.

"It's okay. Things are much better now. I have a job I love, steady income, and food on the table." He tipped his head at the pile of books on the counter. "It's satisfying to share my good fortune."

"That's really nice," she said, holding his gaze a moment longer than necessary. She stepped back and cleared her throat, remembering the gift Nick had given him last Christmas Eve, the one she'd made him promise to use. "So, does that mean you believe in magic now?"

Benny laughed. "No. I wouldn't go that far. I still think you make your own magic."

Laura wasn't about to disagree. She'd made her own way in the world as well. If she'd waited for some fairy godmother to wave her wand and turn a pumpkin into a coach, she'd be old and gray with a yard full of rotten pumpkins. "Why don't I ring these up for you," she said, moving behind the counter.

She could feel his eyes watching her. Rather than making her uncomfortable, however, his long, lingering glances made her wish she'd brushed her hair instead of pulling it up in a make-shift bun. And why hadn't she taken time with her make-up this morning instead of rushing out with only a swipe of mascara and blush? Something about the way he looked at her, however, made her think he liked her just fine the way she was.

She rang up the surprise box. It was the first one they'd sold. "I hope your friend likes this," she said, realizing afterward that it might be perceived as a leading question. It was none of her business who he was buying it for.

"I'm sure she will. It's for my neighbor Sally. I saw the article you wrote about her in your newsletter."

"Sally Sobieski? Oh, well that explains it." She'd thought it was simply a coincidence that he'd dropped in. But if he'd seen her newsletter, then he knew this was her bookstore.

"I wanted to pick up some books for the kids at the shelter anyway and decided to come here and support a local small business."

Laura nodded. "I wish more people felt that way."

"I'll be happy to spread the word." Benny watched her bag the surprise box. "Have you sold a lot of these?"

"To be honest, you're the first."

"It'll catch on," he assured her. "To tell the truth, I'd buy one every month if you had a subscription program."

Laura mulled it over. It was a good idea. A *great* idea, as a matter of fact. "I think you have something there," she said, wondering why she hadn't thought of it herself. "People love getting things in the mail."

She ran his credit card, then handed it back. Their fingers brushed for a moment and the casual touch sent a tingle through her body that caught her off guard.

Benny signed the newsletter mailing list on the counter, adding his email, home address and telephone number. "Put me down as your first customer for the monthly subscription boxes."

"I will," she said, handing him the bag of books.

He thanked her and turned to leave, waving to Ivy on his way out the door. Laura watched him go, wishing they'd had a chance to talk a bit longer. She'd seen the way he'd looked at her ring. Why hadn't she told him it was a gift from a friend and not an engagement ring?

The truth was, she'd avoided relationships for so long it was second nature. She didn't want to trust or depend on anyone only to be let down again.

"He's kind of cute," Ivy said, startling Laura.

"When did you sneak up on me?"

Ivy chuckled. "When you were staring at that man's butt as he walked away."

"Was not." A smile curled her lips. "Okay, I was admiring his broad shoulders." Nah, she was checking out all of him.

"I heard his idea about the subscription boxes. I like it."

"Me too." Laura decided to grill Ivy for more information. "I hear he knows your friend Sally."

"Yeah. Funny thing, she's been talking about her neighbor for months now. How good he is to her, fixing things and taking her shopping. If you listen to her, he hung the moon and the stars. Guess he's one of the good guys, huh?"

"Yeah," Laura stared out the window where he'd disappeared. Hadn't Nick said those exact words? "Guess so."

Chapter Seven

Benny waved to the receptionist and made his way to the children's playroom. Gabe spotted Benny the moment he walked in the door. He ran and jumped into his arms. Benny tousled the boy's hair, then set him down gently. "You've gotten taller since I last saw you. How you doing, Sport?"

Gabe stood up taller and crinkled his nose. "My name's not Sport. Did you forget already?"

"No. I know your name. Abraham, right?"

Gabe laughed. "No!"

"Theodore?"

"No!"

"Tyrannosaurus Rex?"

Gabe curled his fists into tiny claws and roared.

"Spoken like a true dinosaur," Benny said. He reached into the bag and pulled out the book he'd set on top.

Gabe's face lit up a smile. "For me?"

"Yep, for you. Open it and see a surprise."

When Gabe opened the book, a dinosaur popped up from between the pages. "Oh cool!" He turned another page and exclaimed at each pop-up dinosaur. "I love it. It's like magic," he said, giving Benny an impulsive hug.

There he goes with the magic again, Benny

thought. He pointed to the bag. "I have some books for the other kids here, but that one's special for you." He turned to the inside cover. "See? I put your name in there."

With exquisite care, Gabe sounded out each word. "To. Gabe. F. Fa. From. Your. Fer. Friend. Benny." He smiled at Benny. "You didn't forget my name."

"Nope. Won't forget you ever, kiddo." It amazed Benny how something as simple as a pop-up book gave the boy so much pleasure. No question Gabe tugged at his heartstrings. He'd give the kid the world if he could.

"Hey Gabe," he said. "Did you know there's a place that has real-life dinosaur bones on display?"

Gabe's eyes opened wide with wonder. "Really?"

"Yep. It's called a museum. Would you like to see it?"

Gabe jumped up and down, barely containing his excitement. "Yes, please? I want to see the dinosaurs like in the book."

"Okay, let's go." He took Gabe's hand and walked toward the front desk. "I'm taking Gabe to the museum for a few hours."

The receptionist shot to her feet and stopped him. "You can't just walk out with one of the children!"

Benny stopped. "Oh, do I have to sign him out or something?"

The receptionist looked at him like he'd grown an extra head. "You need to clear it with Ms. Miller." She pointed to the hallway. "I'll tell her you're coming."

Benny made his way to Ms. Miller's office. Gabe skipped along beside him, his eyes bright with eagerness.

"Come in," a woman called when Benny knocked

on the door. She stood to greet him. "Mr. Carter it is, right?"

"Yes, ma'am. Call my Benny."

Before he could explain further, however, Gabe chattered. "Benny's my friend. He brought me books and said there's a dinosaur, a real dinosaur at the museum. Can I go, please? Can I?"

Carol knelt until she was face to face with Gabe. "We'll talk about it, okay? Would you wait outside for a few moments while I talk to Mr. Carter?"

Gabe blinked back tears. "It has real dinosaurs," he mumbled under his breath as he walked away. It broke Benny's heart to see how readily the boy accepted disappointment. He could have kicked himself for being the cause of it and not checking first to make sure it would be okay before getting Gabe's hopes up.

"I'm sorry if I crossed the line." He tried to explain himself to the social worker. "I thought maybe I could be like a Big Brother or something to Gabe. You know, take him places and stuff."

Carol stood and brushed the hem of her dress. "This isn't the Big Brother Organization. We're a shelter for neglected and abused children. I can't let one of them go off with a stranger, no matter how well intentioned, Mr. Carter."

"Call me Benny."

She nodded. "Benny. I'm sure you understand."

"Yes, but I hate to see the boy disappointed."

Carol took a deep breath and glanced toward the doorway. It was evident that she felt the same way but was bound by rules and regulations. She chewed her bottom lip thoughtfully. "How about...I get a group of children together for a field trip to the museum. I'll need chaperones, and if you'd like to volunteer—"

"Yes," Benny shouted before she could finish. "That's a great idea. It would have to be a Saturday because I work. Of course, I could probably take a day off, but…"

Carol smiled. "It's okay. We'll plan the outing for next Saturday. That will give me time to round up a few other volunteers and make the arrangements."

Benny turned toward the door. "Can I tell Gabe?"

Benny opened the door of Carol's office and called Gabe inside. "I'm afraid I have some bad news," he said. "I forgot to check with Ms. Carol before saying we could go to the museum. I was too impulsive."

Gabe's lower lip trembled. "What's impulsive?"

"That's when you do something without checking first," Benny explained. "But it's okay," he said. "We decided to go to the museum as a group. You and your friends will all be able to see the dinosaurs and lots of other things as well."

Gabe pursed his lips. "Are you sure? Don't be explosive again."

"Impulsive," Benny said. "And I'm not. I promise. I checked with Ms. Carol first and she said it would be okay."

Gabe hesitated, then asked. "Are you coming too?"

"Yes. And Ms. Carol is going to arrange for some other grown-ups to join us on our trip."

Gabe looked at Carol with large, innocent eyes. "Maybe Miss Laura can come, too."

Benny couldn't help but smile. That sounded like a wonderful plan to him.

Carol looked from Benny to Gabe and back, one eyebrow lifted. "We'll see," she said.

And that was good enough for Benny. He resisted the urge to give Gabe a high five. Of course, the boy couldn't have known how much Benny enjoyed Laura's company. It was just a coincidence—a coincidence that happened to work out in Benny's favor.

****

The next Saturday Benny was filled with anticipation. He had no right to look forward to seeing Laura as much as he did, but he couldn't deny his feelings. When he arrived at Hyatt House, she was already there, dressed in a blue linen dress that looked both casual and comfortable enough for a day wrangling children at the museum.

Carol had the children lined up single file. One by one they boarded a minivan with the Hyatt House logo on the side. Gabe tried to break free. "Can I ride with Benny?" he shouted.

Benny saw Carol shake her head and urge Gabe forward. He joined the rest of the children in the van, but his lower lip puckered outward and he cast sad, puppy-dog eyes in Benny's direction.

Benny winked and curled his hands into dinosaur claws, mouthing a roar, turning Gabe's frown into a smile of delight. Benny turned and saw Laura staring at him. "I was just…"

She nodded and a slow smile curved her lips. "I know."

"Why don't you ride with me?" he suggested. "No sense taking two cars." On second thought, he added. "Unless you have somewhere to rush off to after the museum."

"No. That sounds fine."

He led her to his car and opened the passenger door

before she could reach for the handle. He stopped himself from buckling the seat belt around her, aware that would be pushing chivalry too far. He closed her door, then went around to the driver's seat and started the car. When the Hyatt House van pulled out, he slipped in behind it, driving carefully. After all, he had precious cargo in the passenger seat.

Benny glanced at Laura. "Gabe wanted you to chaperone," he said. "He adores you."

"Gabe's a sweet kid. He thinks the world of you as well."

Benny nodded. "He reminds me of my youngest nephew Timmy. Unmistakably as cute and precocious." He took a deep breath and let it out with a sigh. "I haven't seen Timmy or the others in over a year."

"Why's that?"

Benny shrugged one shoulder. "They're all scattered across the country—my brothers, sisters, nieces and nephews. Even my parents. They retired to Florida. They all have jobs or school schedules, so it's hard to find a time and place where we can all meet. We video chat," he said. "But virtually getting together isn't the same. If I hadn't lost my job, I'd have flown out to at least visit my parents over the holidays, but I had to change my plans. I miss the family gatherings, home cooking, parties, and game nights."

Laura gave him a strange, almost pitying look.

"It's okay," he said. "Now that I'm working again, I'm going to visit each and every one of them. I have to keep my standing as favorite uncle."

"Only uncle," she reminded him, and they both had a good laugh.

Benny was amazed at how comfortable it was to

talk with Laura. The conversation flowed without effort. Maybe he'd shared too much, but something about her made it easy to confide his deepest feelings and emotions.

When they arrived at the museum, Carol pulled Benny aside as the children were filing out of the van. "Gabe is very attached to you," she said. "Maybe too attached."

"Is that a bad thing?" Benny asked. "Doesn't every boy need a male role model in his life? Especially when his real father is absent."

"You're not his father." Carol took a deep breath. "I was going to tell you next week, but there's a foster family that's ready to take Gabe in. They're a lovely couple, and Gabe is lucky. I think you need to make a clean break after this to give him time to adjust and bond with his new family."

Benny wasn't so sure. It broke his heart to think of making a clean break with Gabe, but Carol was the expert. If she said it was for the boy's well-being, he'd have to trust her judgment.

Laura was waiting for Benny to catch up, when he returned.

"Everything all right?" she asked as he stepped beside her.

"Yeah," he said, but the furrowed brow and clenched fist gave him away. Something had changed in the few moments he'd spent talking to Carol. Benny looked as if he'd been kicked in the stomach. "What is it?"

He shook his head slowly. "A moment ago, I found out Gabe is going into a foster home."

Laura blinked. A foster home? Her heart sank, but

she put on a brave face. "That's a good thing," she said. "Every child deserves to be part of a family, a place to feel protected and loved." That was something Miss Edna always said. Everything else was simply trimming—a nice house, money, trips to Disney. Those were great, but love was the number one requisite.

"*I* love him," Benny murmured, as if just now realizing the truth of what he was saying.

"I know you do. But you're in no position to give him what he needs—a home, two parents, and security. You're finally getting back on your own feet. Besides," she added. "Hyatt House has strict rules about single parents. There's no way they'd let you foster, let alone *adopt* a child."

Benny lowered his voice to a whisper, "Carol said I need to make a clean break."

The way he'd choked on his words, made Laura ache to reach out and wrap him in a comforting hug. But before she could give in to the urge, Gabe ambled back.

The child took Benny's hand and asked, "Where are the dinosaurs?"

"We're getting there, Gabe. Be patient and listen to the tour guide. I promise we'll see the dinosaurs soon."

"Okay," Gabe said. "I'm just feeling so, so…explosive!"

Laura glanced from Gabe to Benny, who chuckled. "Impulsive, not explosive. That's his new word for the week."

Laura smiled. They really were cute together. If Miss Edna was still in charge, perhaps things could be different, but she wasn't, and Carol was right. Better to make a clean break and give Gabe a chance to adjust to a new home.

When Benny talked about growing up in a large, loving family, she couldn't help feeling a twinge of old jealousy. He'd had the life she'd always wanted. The closest thing she'd had to a family was Miss Edna, who might have been the family Laura so fervently wished for, if only she hadn't gotten sick. Things just hadn't worked out in their favor.

Gabe still had a chance, however, and she was happy for him, even while she acknowledged that it would break Benny's heart to see him go.

They finally reached the dinosaur section, and Gabe gasped when he spotted the first dinosaur replica. "That's a stegosaurus," he exclaimed. "They eat plants."

He stopped at a towering dinosaur skeleton, gazing upward in awe. "Whoa." He turned to Benny. "Is that real?"

Before Benny could do more than nod, the tour guide spoke up. "This 42-foot long, 657-million-year-old dinosaur is one of the most complete and best-preserved Tyrannosaurus rex skeletons in the world."

Gabe reached out. "Can I touch it?"

"No," they all shouted at once, causing Gabe to jerk his hand back. He giggled, and then turned full circle, taking in each dinosaur on display. "This is my best day *ever*!"

Benny glanced at Laura and they shared a smile, for all the world, looking like proud parents.

****

Later that day, once everyone had returned to Hyatt House, Laura cornered Carol. "What was that all about?"

"What?"

"This, this…this chaperone thing with Benny. Are you into matchmaking all of a sudden?"

"First of all," Carol said, holding up one finger. "Gabe specifically asked if you could chaperone. And second, what's wrong with spending time with someone who cares as much about the children as you do?"

Laura flipped her hair back. "I'm not interested." She didn't need anyone. They'd only disappoint. Experience had proven the only person she could count on was herself.

"Is that why you started wearing that fake engagement ring?"

"It's not fake."

"So, you *are* engaged?"

"No. I mean the ring isn't fake. It belonged to Edna Hyatt. She gave it to me to remind me…" Tears stung her eyes. "To remind me that I was loved."

Carol reached out and gave her hand a gentle squeeze. "I'm sorry. I know Edna loved you like her own daughter." She eyed the ring. "The ring seems like a shield you've put up to keep men away."

"I don't…"

Carol raised an eyebrow.

"Okay, maybe I do. It's easier than having to turn down dates."

"Why would you turn down a date? What's the harm in going to dinner and a movie every now and then?"

Laura blew out a breath. "Because dinner and a movie lead to more and before you know it someone is wanting to be in an exclusive relationship and a commitment and…"

"And a family?"

Damn, Carol knew her too well. "Yeah, I guess."

"Look," Carol said. "I'm your friend, not your psychologist, but even I can see that your fear of abandonment is keeping you from being happy and fulfilled."

Laura crossed her hands over her chest. "Who says I'm not happy?"

"I'm not saying you can't be happy and single at the same time. If that's your choice."

Laura didn't respond. She didn't want to argue, but Carol had hit one of her hot buttons. Why did everyone think she needed a man in her life to be happy and fulfilled?

Carol shrugged. "I didn't mean any harm. It's...Benny seems like such a nice guy. I thought the two of you might have some things in common, and you could lower that shield."

As much as she hated to admit it, Laura suspected Carol might be right. She *did* feel attracted to Benny. If anything, it gave her more reason to avoid him.

****

However, it became harder and harder to avoid running into Benny. Some days she'd see him at the shelter and other days he'd drop by the bookstore. Then when Sally Sobieski's book release party rolled around, of course he showed up at the book signing as well.

Laura had ordered a cake from Beverley's Bake Shop and placed congratulatory balloons around the bookstore. Ivy was there, as well as Sally's friend Judy and all the members of the writers' group. Several other interested people stopped in after reading the sign Laura had placed in the window advertising a new author's book.

Laura noticed one of her regular customers, Lou Burton, spending extra time at Sally's table. While she signed books from a stack on the table, she spent time talking to each person. Lou handed her the books to sign and brought her water every once in a while. Apparently, after being soundly rejected by Ivy nearly every morning at the coffee station, he'd turned his attention to Sally.

Although Laura couldn't hear their conversation, Sally's cheeks blossomed to a bright pink flush. "Look at those two," she said when Benny moved to stand beside her.

Benny nodded. "He's been spending a lot of time at the apartment. To be honest, I'm a little jealous because Sally hardly ever calls me anymore to fix something or help her with her computer. I think I've been replaced."

Laura chuckled. "I guess you're never too old to fall in love, huh? This could be a whole new chapter for Sally to add to her memoirs."

"Or maybe she could start a new book," he suggested. "Something like *Second Chance at Love.*"

The word *love* snagged in Laura's mind, so she almost missed Benny's question.

"Have you ever thought about it?" he asked.

"Huh?" Laura shook her head. "Thought about what?"

"Writing a book? Obviously, you love books. I was wondering if you'd ever thought of writing one."

"Maybe," she said. But she knew that wasn't the truth. She didn't believe in happy endings, so what would she write about? Her life? That was too depressing. No one would want to read it. "What about you?" she asked.

Benny shook his head. "Nope. I don't have the imagination for it. I'll leave writing to the experts."

They both joined Sally at the table as she began to open her gifts. When she came to Benny's gift, she threw her hands up in delight. "I love it," she said, admiring each item as she removed them from the box.

"You can thank Ivy for the suggestion," Benny said, "And Laura for the gift box idea." The look he gave her made her toes curl.

Sally reached for the book and ran her fingers over the soft leather cover. "It's beautiful. Thank you, Benny."

He leaned down and kissed the top of her head. The gesture made Laura melt. *Such a sweet and thoughtful man.* Any woman would be grateful to have a caring man like that in her life.

But no sooner had the thought come than she brushed it aside. Maybe other women needed a man to coddle and care for them, but not her. She had herself, her friends, and her bookstore. That was all she needed. All she'd ever need.

Chapter Eight

Benny made it a habit to stop by the community center on the first Saturday of the month to drop off a donation for the food pantry. Now that he had a steady job, it was his way of paying it forward. He glanced around. The sights and smells of the community center brought him right back to the day when he'd reached his lowest point. He still remembered how he'd felt...the sense of hopelessness and hunger.

How things had changed.

Today, he had a job he loved and money in his pocket. He even saved up a little nest egg for a deposit on a house in the near future, all because he'd answered a few questions in a notebook.

A clap on his back broke his reverie. "Benny, my friend. Good to see you."

Benny turned. "Nick, is that you?"

He hardly recognized Nick in street clothes. His snow-white hair was slicked back, and his beard was pulled into a ponytail held with a rubber band. He looked like Santa's cooler brother, the one who would more likely jump on a Harley than a reindeer-driven sleigh.

"In the flesh," he said with that distinctive laugh. "I'm making egg deliveries today. What brings you here?"

Benny shuffled his feet. "Oh, I just stopped by to, um…"

Nick smiled. "Make a donation to the food pantry?"

"Yeah, someone told you, huh? It's not much, but my way of paying back."

Nick nodded. "Not necessary but appreciated. Every little bit helps." He jerked his head to the side. "As long as you're here, want to help me with some of those egg crates?"

"Sure." Benny walked with Nick out to his truck, a green pick-up that had seen better days. Holly Hill Farms was painted on the outside. Inside were cartons of eggs in a metal crate secured to the bed of the truck.

"Wow," Benny said. "How many chickens do you have?"

Nick hefted a crate of eggs. "Never really counted. Couple hundred, I'd say. Rhode Island Reds because they're hardy and lay eggs all winter long. Those hens lay more eggs than my wife and I could eat if we ate eggs for breakfast, lunch, and dinner every day of the week."

Benny lifted a crate and followed Nick inside. "So, you donate them?"

"Not all," Nick said. "We have regular customers. The food co-op has a standing order for eggs, as well as two local restaurants and an organic food market. That still leaves plenty of eggs to donate, both here and to the shelter."

Benny nodded. "I've been meaning to ask you something, Nick."

Nick set the crate down and straightened. "Ask away. I'm an open book."

An open book? Was that a clue? Benny didn't want to come right out and ask, not if it meant another lecture about magic boxes and wishes. But he had to know. "How do you feel about fruitcake?" he finally asked, watching Nick's reaction.

Nick winked and patted his tummy. "Love it!"

"Someone left me a fruitcake from Beverley's Bake Shop."

"You're a lucky man. Beverley makes the best fruitcake in town. People from all over the country order her Magical Fruitcake for Christmas."

"I had the opportunity to meet her a few weeks back. She's a lovely woman."

"Oh, that she is," Nick said with a smile. "That she is."

Benny decided not to push it any further. Maybe he didn't really want to know the truth about magical boxes and magical fruitcakes. Maybe a small part of him wanted to believe in magic after all.

Speaking of magic, he couldn't resist asking. "Did you leave that book on my doorstep last Christmas?"

"Book?" Nick shook his head from side to side. "Hmmm…was it a good one?"

The twinkle in the man's eyes told Benny he knew exactly what the notebook had done. "Yeah, it was a good one all right. Read it from cover to cover."

Before Benny could ask any further questions, Nick turned to leave. "We can talk later," he said. "I have more deliveries to make."

Benny held up his rack of eggs. "What should I do with these?"

"Oh, would you mind dropping them off at the shelter for me?"

"The shelter?"

"Yeah, if it's not out of your way."

"I guess not, but..." Of course, he didn't mind. Gabe wouldn't be there since he was living with a foster family now, but Benny hoped to run into Laura.

Their paths had crossed over the last few weeks, and while Benny was always glad to see her, he resigned himself to keep their relationship platonic. Platonic was better than no relationship at all.

"Hey Nick?"

He turned and cocked his head.

"Do you love your job?" Benny asked.

Nick smiled. "Wouldn't trade it for the world."

Benny nodded. "Thought so."

Sure enough he'd left the notebook. Not that it mattered. The end result was the same. Good fortune was one thing, but he certainly wouldn't call it magic.

****

Benny had every intention of dropping the eggs off at Hyatt House, then swinging by the bookstore. He'd been a regular customer, lately. Sometimes Laura was working behind the counter, and sometimes he'd catch a glimpse of her in her office. She always smiled and waved, and that alone was worth the price of a hard cover book or two. Just thinking of Laura brought a smile to his own face.

He dropped the eggs off in the dining room, then turned when he heard his name cried out from across the room. "Mr. Benny, Mr. Benny!" Gabe waved furiously to get his attention.

Benny whirled around, surprised to see Gabe back at the shelter. His smile faltered when he saw Gabe's arm in a cast. Another little boy was signing the cast, his tongue sticking out the side of his mouth as he wrote with slow, careful strokes.

Benny rushed to Gabe's side and went down on one knee. "What happened to you?"

Gabe's face was as proud as only a five-year old sporting his first cast could be. "I broked my arm. Then I went to the hospital and went to sleep and when I woked up I had this cast on." He held up a purple felt-tip pen. "Want to sign it?"

Benny took several deep breaths, trying not to let his anger show. His first thought was that Gabe had been abused by someone in his new foster family and if Benny got his hands on the culprit...

He tried to keep his voice calm. "But what happened before you broke your arm, Gabe?"

"Oh. I climbed a tree. It was so, so high, but I wasn't ascared. I kept climbing up and up and up. And then it broke, and I fell, down and down and down."

Benny took the pen. "I'm sorry buddy. Did it hurt much?"

Gabe tried his best to look brave, but his bottom lip quivered. "Maybe some."

"Where were...?"

He was interrupted by a strong throat clearing sound, and only then did he see Laura. He'd been too concerned with Gabe's injury to notice her there at the table.

"He's fine," Laura assured him. "And he's been anxious to see you."

Benny let out a slow breath, feeling his heartbeat return to normal. Maybe he'd jumped to conclusions. He still wanted to know why Gabe was climbing trees unsupervised, but he'd deal with that later. He finished signing Gabe's cast with a flourish, then handed the pen back.

Gabe patted the seat beside him. "Want to sit with us?"

"Sure." Benny settled between Gabe and Laura, only then noticing the dishes on the table. "Have you eaten?"

"Yeah, and Miss Laura said if I ate all my lunch, I could have apple pie. Want some?"

"Sounds good to me."

Laura held up her hand. "I'll get it."

Grateful for a few moments alone with Gabe, he turned his attention to the boy. "When did you get back?"

"Last night. I asked Miss Carol if you could come visit, but she said it was too late, and I had to get my jammas on. But then she read me a book about the moon, and I fell asleep." Gabe took a deep breath. "Then I got up and had pancakes, and Miss Laura came over, and we ate lunch, and now you're here! It's my best day ever."

"Mine too," Benny said, wrapping an arm around Gabe and pulling him close. "And you're my best surprise."

Gabe nodded his head up and down. "Like magic, huh?"

"Well, not exactly."

Laura came back to the table with two dishes of apple pie. She put one in front of each of them. "He's been obsessed with your magic box. That's all he talks about." She turned those amazing eyes on Benny, causing his heart to skip a beat. "He wanted to know if you've made another wish in your magic box."

Benny tried to remember how old he was when he stopped believing in magic. Had the world lost some of its sparkle that day? Had he become a little less hopeful and slightly more jaded? He thought about the magic box and how much the child inside him yearned to believe again, even if the adult knew better.

Gabe talked around a mouthful of pie. "Did you wish for more fruitcake?"

Benny chuckled. The kid had a memory like an elephant. "No," he said with a smile.

"What are you going to wish for in your magic box?"

Benny wasn't sure how to respond to that. Before he could figure out what to say, Gabe hit him with a barrage of questions. "Maybe you could ask for a dog. Do you have a dog?"

"No."

"Do you have a house?"

"No, I live in an apartment."

"Do you have a bedtime?

Benny shook his head.

"How come?"

"Because I'm an adult and can stay up as late as I want."

Gabe thought about it, a frown on his face. "But…who takes care of you?"

Benny opened his mouth to say something, then closed it again. Good question. It wasn't as if he needed someone to take care of him, but the thought had been on his mind. He did need someone to care *about* him.

He'd once heard that the most basic human need after food and shelter was someone who was happy to see you when you came home, someone who cared about your health, happiness, and desires.

"I take care of myself," Benny said, perhaps a little more gruffly than he intended.

"Why? Doesn't anyone love you?"

Ouch. That was all the push Benny needed. He'd been playing with an idea, but Gabe's question convinced him there was only one possible wish to come next.

Clearing his throat, Benny changed the subject, putting an end to Gabe's questions. He ruffled Gabe's hair. "I think you've grown a foot since I've seen you!"

Gabe looked down at his two feet, causing Benny to let out a laugh.

"Benny?"

He shook his head and turned his attention to Laura. "Hmm?"

"Where did you get the eggs?"

"Eggs?" Benny blinked. "Oh, the eggs. I ran into Nick, and he asked me to drop them off here."

Laura nodded, but suspicion clouded her face.

"You don't think he arranged all this, do you?"

She shrugged. "Coincidence, I guess."

Coincidence or not, Benny was glad to be in the right place at the right time, not only because Gabe was here, but Laura as well.

Her voice softened, "Nick told me you've been making donations to the community center kitchen. And according to Carol, you've been dropping books and puzzles for the kids here."

Benny shrugged. "It's not a big deal."

Laura reached out and rested her hand on his arm. "Yes. It is." She held his gaze for a moment, then lowered her eyes and stepped back, but his skin still tingled where she'd touched him.

"Do you mind helping me put those eggs away?" Benny asked.

Laura gave him a quizzical look, but when Benny glanced at Gabe and tilted his head, she got the hint.

As soon as they were out of hearing range, Benny turned to Laura, his fists clenched. "Do you know how he broke his arm? He fell out of a tree. Wasn't anyone watching him?"

Laura shook her head. "All I know is what Carol told me. Apparently, the foster mother was distracted by a phone call. She thought Gabe would be okay in the yard for a few minutes. She wasn't used to little boys and how quickly they can get into trouble."

"That's no excuse. It could have been much worse."

Laura reached out and squeezed his hand. "Yes, but it wasn't."

His face grew more solemn.

"Unfortunately, the foster parents decided they couldn't handle a boy his age. They sent him back."

"Good," Benny snapped.

"No. Not good" Emotion strangled her voice. "It was a mistake, but it's more of a mistake to let a child start to feel safe and secure, then tear the rug out from under them." She took a deep breath. "I know people hear horror stories about foster care, but the truth is that most foster homes are made up of loving, caring people who truly want to help. They don't realize how much of a commitment fostering a child can be—how much time, patience and money it actually takes."

She felt that old familiar pang of hopelessness, abandonment, and loss. "I was there once," she blurted out. "I grew up in the same shelter where Gabe is now."

Benny blinked. "What?"

"I was shuffled from one foster home to another until I was too old to be placed anymore. I know what it's like to feel abandoned, unwanted and unloved."

Benny reached out and placed a comforting hand on her shoulder. His silence helped her find the words she hadn't shared with anyone before. "After a while you start to build up a shell to protect yourself from the pain. The shell gets thicker and thicker until you can't trust anyone but yourself."

Benny's eyes went soft with sympathy. "I'm sorry you had to go through that."

"I don't want that to happen to Gabe."

"I don't, either."

Laura blew out a breath, feeling lighter for having shared her shame. Only now she realized she had nothing to be ashamed of. She wasn't unlovable. She hadn't been tossed away like garbage left by the side of the road. It wasn't her fault, any more than it was Gabe's fault he'd been sent back to the shelter.

"Everyone has the same needs," she said. "The need to be loved, sheltered, and protected."

Benny nodded, and that struck a chord in her. She felt a rush of anger swirl in the pit of her stomach. "You wouldn't know," she said, hearing the bitterness in her own voice. "You grew up in a perfect home with perfect parents and a white picket fence. You don't know what it's like to want a family more than anything else in the whole world."

He squeezed her hand, and she felt the ring pressed between them. He released her hand and gestured to the ring on her finger. "You have that within your grasp now," he said. "You can put the past behind you now and move on to a bright future and a white picket fence."

Laura didn't correct his assumption. It was easy to let Benny believe she was engaged. She knew telling him the truth would be the right thing to do, but the shell she'd built to protect herself was too strong. Somewhere deep down inside she believed if she let down her guard, she'd only be hurt in the end.

"You're right," she said. "I can put the past behind me now."

If only that were true.

One thing was true, however. She didn't want Gabe growing up with the same insecurities she had. She didn't want him getting lost on the foster home merry-go-round. That's why when Benny went back to sit with Gabe, Laura said her goodbyes and made her way to Carol's office.

"I want to adopt Gabe," she said without preamble.

Carol took a deep breath, then blew it out with a sigh. "You know that's not possible, Laura. There are rules we have to follow here. Children can only be adopted by two-parent families."

"That wasn't always the case," Laura argued. "When Edna was in charge, her only rule was that every child deserved to be loved."

Carol pushed some files to the side of her desk, avoiding Laura's eyes. "Edna's not in charge anymore, I'm afraid. The corporation makes the rules."

Laura's stomach clenched. *The Corporation.* "I know and they've sucked the heart right out of the shelter."

"Laura." Carol's tone left no room for argument.

"They're doing what they feel is right. They only want what's best for the children."

Laura blinked back tears. She twisted the ring on her finger, an idea forming. "What if I was engaged?"

Carol glanced at the ring and lifted an eyebrow. "To Edna Hyatt?"

Laura had forgotten she'd told Carol that Edna had given her the ring. That was the problem with lies. They had a way of backfiring. "Okay, so I'm not engaged, but maybe we could find a way around the rules. If Edna was here, she'd say that a single-parent home was better than no home at all. She'd say that love overshadows rules and regulations."

"Edna's not here."

"I know."

"Besides," Carol said. "Even if you were engaged, you couldn't even fill out the paperwork until you were legally married."

Laura heaved a sigh of resignation. There was no husband or fiancé in her future. Even if there were, it might be too late to adopt Gabe.

Carol put a finger to her lips. "But you gave me an idea. We might have a way around this."

Laura's heart lurched. "Really?"

Carol nodded. "You're not the only one who cares about Gabe. I do too. I'd love to see him placed in a happy home."

"So, you'd bend the rules?"

Carol shook her head. "No, I don't have the authority to do that. But your *engagement* ring gave me an idea. There's someone else who loves Gabe."

Before Laura could ask, Carol lifted her pencil, as if conjuring the name out of thin air. "Benjamin Carter.

He's nuts over the kid."

"So?"

Carol shook her head. "For crying out loud, Laura. You own a bookstore. Don't you read romance novels? Do I have to spell it out?"

"Apparently."

"A marriage of convenience," she explained. "You guys get married, adopt Gabe and live happily ever after. Or separate, but by then the adoption already would have been finalized and you'd get to keep Gabe."

Laura couldn't believe what she was hearing. She shook her head adamantly. "No. Absolutely not."

"Why not? It's the perfect solution. A win-win if you ask me."

"First off," Laura said, tapping her index finger on her other hand. "I have no desire to get married. Second, if I did, I wouldn't marry a stranger. And third…" She stopped, rolling the idea around in her mind and realizing she didn't have as many arguments against it as she thought. "Third, it's a stupid plot device, not something that happens in real life."

Carol held up her hands in mock surrender. "Okay, it was only a suggestion."

"Well," Laura said. "I appreciate the suggestion, but that's not going to happen." She stopped, realizing they were both on the same side, although each coming at it from different angles. "What's going to happen to Gabe?"

"We have another foster home lined up for him. I'm hoping this one works out better."

Laura sighed. "I hope so, too." She had a feeling it wouldn't, but that was probably her own past creeping up to haunt her.

Chapter Nine

Benny spent the afternoon with Gabe, then stopped at a florist's shop on the way home and picked up a potted plant for Sally. When she opened the door, her eyes lit up with delight. "Oh Benny, thank you so much. I know exactly where I'm going to put this."

She gestured for him to follow her inside. "You're just in time to join me for dinner." She pointed to the stove. "I made a big pot of beef stew and was planning on bringing a dish over to you anyway, but since you're here we can eat together."

Benny followed her inside and was captivated by the mouthwatering aroma of stewed meat and gravy. "Smells delicious," he said taking a seat. He placed the plant in the center of the table. "The lady at the shop said it was an African violet. It reminded me of you."

Sally spooned soup into two bowls and brought them to the table. "Well, purple is my favorite color."

Benny dipped his spoon into the stew, then blew across the surface. The fragrant steam sent his taste buds tingling. "Mmm...this is delicious."

"Brunswick stew," Sally said. "It was Oliver's favorite."

"How long has he been gone?"

"Four years in June, and I miss him every single day." Her lips turned up in a sad smile. "We had many good years, Ollie and I. He was my best friend and the love of my life."

"I'm sorry."

Sally wiped a tear from her eye. "Don't be. I have no regrets. We lived life to the fullest. I miss him dearly, but I'm luckier than most people to have found someone to love and share my life."

Benny wondered what it would be like to have someone to come home to, someone to share his days and nights. He wondered what it would be like not to feel lonely in a crowd full of people, knowing that someone was beside him, supporting him and having his back at all times.

Sally offered to refill his bowl, but Benny shook his head. "I think I've had enough, thank you."

Sally tilted her head. "Can I ask you a question?"

"Sure, ask away."

"Well, I was wondering if you've given any thought to making another wish."

Why was everyone so obsessed with his wishes? "Maybe," he admitted. "Not that I believe in magic. But I guess it's a good way to set my intention and focus on what I want out of life. "

"Look what happened last time," she said. "You wished for the perfect job and that's exactly what you got."

"Yes, but it wasn't dropped in my lap. I had to work for it. You make your own magic in this world." He winked at her. "And with the help of some friends, that's exactly what I did."

Sally patted his arm. "If you say so. Personally, I prefer to believe in magic."

"Oh? So, tell me, if you were given a magic box,

what would you wish for? A new car? A big house? Hitting the lottery?"

Sally smiled. "I'd wish to be twenty all over again, to meet and fall in love with Ollie and live our life in exactly the same way."

"Exactly the same?"

She nodded. "Yes. I wouldn't change a thing."

That gave Benny plenty to think about as he returned to his apartment and put his leftovers in the refrigerator. Imagine living a life with no regrets, wanting to spend it with the same person you'd already spent a lifetime loving.

Benny remembered Laura saying that everyone had a need to be loved, sheltered and protected. Not only children.

He'd considered wishing for a house, but a big house would only make him feel more alone. Besides, he didn't want to leave Sally behind.

As long as he was working, he could keep putting money aside for a new house one day. But love—the kind of love Sally had shared with her husband—that was what he really wanted.

Everyone had someone to love. Everyone but him. As if he needed convincing, Queen's song came on the radio urging him to find somebody to love. Which is why, when he was alone that evening, shortly before the clock struck midnight, Benny sat at his kitchen table with a slip of paper in front of him. He tapped the candy-cane pen against his lips, thinking carefully.

He knew what he was going to wish for—to love and be loved. But how to phrase the wish? He'd learned his lesson last time not to over think his wish. As Nick said, he should trust the box. So even though one person's face came to mind, he refused to ask for a certain type of woman—hair, height, or weight—but instead tried to think about what kind of person would complement his personality and fit comfortably into his life. He thought about the journal and how many questions he'd answered before realizing what kind of job best suited him. But that was a job. He couldn't place those same criteria on a person. After careful consideration, at the stroke of midnight he wrote simply...

I wish to love and be loved.

Was that a song lyric or a line from a forgotten poem? He closed the box with a solid click. The sound echoed in the silent room. Benny nodded, as if saying a prayer. Maybe these rooms wouldn't be silent much longer.

He stared at the box a few moments, before finally going to bed.

****

After leaving Hyatt House, carrying a birthday cake from Beverley's Bake Shop, Laura stopped to visit Edna who wore a Happy Birthday crown, when she arrived.

Edna poured them hot chocolate and added a smattering of mini marshmallows, "Because it's a special occasion," she said with a smile.

Edna unwrapped the gift Laura brought for her but frowned when she saw it was an eBook reader. "Now how am I going to figure out how to use this contraption?"

"It's easy." Laura showed her the button to turn it on. "Look, and I've already filled it with some of your favorite authors."

Edna's face scrunched up. "I like being able to hold a real book in my hands. You should understand that, owning a bookstore."

"I love books too, but it's the story that counts, not the way it's delivered." She turned the reader around so Edna could see it better, then showed her some of the features. "You can increase the font until you can read it without your glasses."

"Well that's good, since these glasses have a habit of walking away."

"And you can read in bed at night without turning a light on. See? The screen is backlit, which also makes it easier to read."

Edna snorted.

Laura ignored her and pointed out more features, like the built-in dictionary and thesaurus.'

"I guess I could get used to it," Edna said, playing with the buttons.

The clincher came when Laura showed her how many books she'd downloaded onto the reader. Edna turned it over and back again. "Wow, all those books in this little thing?"

"Yep, all your favorite romance authors." She played with the hem of her shirt for a moment. "So, you read a lot of romance books. Have you ever heard of a marriage of convenience?"

"All the time," Edna said. "Why? Are you thinking of writing one?"

"Gosh no. It was a suggestion someone made. That maybe I could get married in order to adopt that little boy I told you about. Gabe."

"Oh? And did this someone have another someone in mind?"

Laura nodded. "Yeah, a man who volunteers at the shelter. He's smitten with the boy as well."

"Does he have a name?"

"Benjamin Carter. Benny."

Edna nodded. "Do you like this Benny fella?"

"He's all right. Kinda cute if you like that Ryan Gosling kind of look."

"I don't know who that is."

Laura waved her hand dismissively. "Doesn't matter. I'm not interested in men."

"You like women? It's okay, if you do. I'm not judging."

"No, I meant I'm not interested in dating. Men *or* women."

"Why?"

Laura shrugged. "For the same reason I don't read romance novels. I don't believe in happily ever after."

"Is that why you wear the ring I gave you on your left hand? To ward off advances from men?"

"Maybe."

Edna ended her questioning and left Laura with sage advice, "Oh honey. Don't let the past destroy your future. Not everyone will disappoint you."

Later, much later, it was past midnight, and Laura couldn't sleep. Evenings were always the worst. During the day her job and friends distracted her, but there was no one to keep her company at night. She couldn't stop thinking about her earlier conversation with Edna.

Reflecting on the woman's wisdom over a cup of Chamomile tea, Laura fiddled with the diamond ring Edna had given her and wondered, what if Edna was right? Did Laura want to spend her life alone rather than risk having her heart broken?

Then Edna had finished with one last question for her to ponder. "Maybe you should give this young man a chance? What can it hurt?"

Only my heart.

Was she that much of a coward?

No.

She finished the last of her tea, rinsed the cup out, and then before she could change her mind, Laura moved the ring from her left hand to her right hand. This time, as if the decision had brought her comfort, she fell into a deep, peaceful sleep.

****

The next morning arrived gray and overcast. Benny dressed and put the coffee on to brew. A knock at the door set his heart stuttering. He stared at the door. Could it be that simple? A wish made and granted overnight?

He went to the door and slowly turned the knob, surprised and somewhat disappointed to see Sally on the other side. She held out a fruitcake and a wrapped package. "Found these on your doorstep," she said. "I figured if I didn't pick them up, someone else would, if you know what I mean."

Benny did. "Thank you." He turned and gestured. "Come on in."

When she stepped inside, Benny closed and locked the door. "Can I get you a cup of coffee? I just made a fresh pot."

She sniffed the air. "It's not decaf, is it?"

"Nope, full strength."

She set the fruit cake on the table and pulled out a chair. "In that case, I'll take a cup. Cream, no sugar."

Benny turned and poured them each a mug, adding

a splash of cream to his neighbor's cup. "Would you like a piece of fruitcake with that?"

"I thought you'd never ask." Sally had already started unwrapping the fruitcake. "This is from the same bakery who delivered it to you last Christmas—Beverley's Bake Shop. Do you think that Santa Claus person sent it?"

Benny nodded.

Sally stopped tugging on the plastic wrap and frowned at Benny. "Why would he do that?"

"I don't know exactly." Benny shrugged. "I didn't believe all this stuff about a magic box. But I made my first wish last Christmas Eve. I wished for a job. Instead I got a fruitcake and a journal full of questions."

"But then you *did* get a job."

"Because of you," Benny said. "You and your friend Judy."

"But you wouldn't have even known about that if you hadn't brought me a piece of your fruitcake. So maybe the box *is* magic. In a roundabout way."

"Very roundabout."

She finished unwrapping the fruitcake while Benny put out plates and silverware. "So," she said, pointing at the wrapped gift in front of him. "What did you wish for this time?"

Heat rushed to his cheeks. "I, um…" He looked away, then mumbled, "I wished for someone to love."

"Hmmmm." Sally gave a thoughtful nod. "I don't think Judy has a niece."

That made Benny laugh. Sally joined in, and the two of them laughed and chatted over fruitcake and coffee.

"Hearing you talk about Ollie did it," Bennie

admitted. "I want that kind of love, the kind that lasts a lifetime."

Sally reached out and squeezed his hand. "Everyone deserves that kind of love. I hope your wish comes true, Benny." She nudged the package across the table. "So, aren't you going to open it?"

"I guess." Benny picked up the package and turned it over a few times. It was smaller than a book. He sighed. The only way to find out was to open it.

"Open it, open it!" Sally clapped her hands together, as if reading his mind.

Benny smiled. Sally seemed more anxious to see what was inside than he was. To be honest, he felt a little nervous. Could finding the love of his life be this simple? He unwrapped the package and stared at the contents.

Sally tipped her head and stared as well, a look of confusion on her face. "A sewing kit?"

Benny turned it over and inspected it. "Yep, a sewing kit." He shook his head. "I have no idea what this means."

The two of them burst out laughing again.

Benny pushed the sewing kit aside. But later, after Sally had left, he tucked it into his briefcase. He couldn't get Nick's words out of his head. *Trust the box*, he'd said. *Trust the box.*

Chapter Ten

Business at the bookstore was slower than normal. It was too early to worry, but if she had another month like last month, Laura would have to come up with a new income stream to supplement the bookstore's cash flow.

She couldn't risk losing the store. It wasn't just a business, it was her life's dream, the thought of which had kept her going through all the hard times. Losing it would be a bitter defeat.

The sound of someone clearing their throat interrupted her thoughts. "Excuse me. Sorry to interrupt."

Laura turned to see Sally Sobieski from the writer's group in the doorway. "No problem, Sally. How can I help you?"

"I'm looking for a special book for someone. He has a birthday coming up and I thought maybe you could help me."

"Did you try looking it up in the online catalog?"

"Yes. And I tried Google, Amazon and eBay too, with no luck."

Laura pulled out a notebook. "What's the name of this book? I have some sources for rare and out-of-print books."

"It's called *The Scent of Moonlight*, by Hester

Carter."

Laura glanced up from the paper she was writing on. "Carter? Like Benjamin Carter?"

"Yes. I forgot you met my friend Benny. Hester was his grandmother. Apparently, she wrote this book of poetry. He mentioned it to me when I told him about my writing group. Said we had something in common."

"And so you do." Laura smiled.

"Anyway, I thought I could get him a copy of the book for his birthday, but it's harder to find than I expected."

"Well, maybe I can track it down. I love a good treasure hunt."

"Thank you so much," Sally said. "His birthday is in June, so we have some time."

"I'll do what I can," she said, ushering Sally to the door. Too late, Laura realized she hadn't logged out of her financial program. She hoped Sally hadn't seen the projected downward graph.

She turned off the laptop and left her office. At the coffee counter, Ivy was filling decorative vases with pink and red flowers surrounding some of their more popular romance novels.

She picked one up and read the back cover—*when her car breaks down on a deserted mountain road, Liz Riley discovers an enchanted cottage where time stands still.*

Good grief. At least it didn't have one of those arranged marriages in it.

"That's a good one," Ivy pointed out.

Laura rolled her eyes. "I'm sure it is, if you believe in magical cottages where dreams come true."

Ivy shrugged. "Everyone has to believe in

something."

Laura believed in something. She believed in hard work and making your own dreams come true. But then she caught sight of another book in the display. The man on the cover looked a lot like Benny—if Benny had a cowboy hat and an attitude. She chuckled, wondering if she'd subconsciously chosen this book for that reason alone.

She hadn't seen Benny in a few weeks and wondered how he was doing. Had he made his second wish, yet? She wondered what it might be. If he showed up at the bookstore driving a Lamborghini, she'd have a pretty good idea.

But no, Benny didn't seem like the kind of guy who'd opt for material things. Hadn't Nick said he was one of the good guys? Just thinking of Nick brought a smile to her face. Nick and Beverley had invited her to dinner that evening, and she was looking forward to a home-cooked meal and good company.

Why did Edna insist she should have friends her own age? She treasured the friends she had, no matter what age they were.

It was still light out when she closed the bookstore. She'd tucked the new cookbook by a popular talk show celebrity in her tote bag. Beverley had dozens of cookbooks, but still got excited when a new one was released. It would make a perfect hostess gift.

She was right. Beverley dove right into the recipe book, highlighting recipes she wanted to try and making notes along the margins. "Don't you think this would be perfect with almond extract?" she asked Laura.

Laura could only nod because Beverley had

already moved onto the next page, mumbling to herself about coconut and fondant.

"Now look what you've done," Nick said with a smile. He patted his stomach. "She'll be trying out new recipes for weeks and I'm the one who will gain weight testing them."

"That's good." Laura chuckled and wrapped her arm around Nick. "Whoever heard of a skinny Santa?"

"You're in a good mood," Nick replied. "Lately you've seemed worried."

"I was," she admitted. "I was concerned about the bookstore," She paused and took a deep breath. "But I think things are about to turn around."

"Oh?"

Laura nodded and smiled. "I got a phone call out of the blue from a local Women's Group. They invited me to speak at their next luncheon. The president of the group told me they have provided grants to local businesswomen in the past. I'll be meeting with them next month at Sun Valley Country Club."

"Sun Valley Country Club? Isn't that where Benny Carter works now?"

"Is it?" Laura frowned. "You don't think?" She shook her head. "No. I'm sure it's a coincidence."

****

Days went by, then weeks. So far, the magic box hadn't delivered the woman of his dreams into his arms. Magic or no magic, Benny was determined to find someone to love. If this wish was anything like the last, it was up to him to take the necessary steps to make his wish come true. That was why he joined several dating sites and spent more hours than he wanted to admit staring at pictures of women who hit all the right notes on paper, but for one reason or another lacked chemistry in person.

It wasn't a total loss. He'd met some lovely women, all of whom fit comfortably into the friend zone. And who couldn't use more friends?

But Benny was searching for the love of his life. Tonight, he was meeting another electronically chosen date. Maybe this would be the one. He tried not to get his hopes up. Instead he focused on what had to be done at work.

The banquet room was booked, and he had back-to-back meetings with people interested in booking it for future events. His mind was occupied which is why he didn't notice the woman until he nearly bumped right into her.

"Oh, excuse me—" He glanced up, then caught his breath. "Melody?"

"Benjamin?" Her eyes widened in surprise. "Fancy meeting you here!"

She reached out and hugged him, as if he was some long-lost friend instead of her jilted lover. Seeing her brought back every emotion, from betrayal to loss to anger. The pain was immense, as if it had happened yesterday. He'd given her his heart and placed a diamond ring on her finger. Before they could make it to the altar, however, he'd caught her with another man and realized everything she'd promised had been a lie.

He was angry, yes, but beneath that anger was remembered emotions. The smell of her perfume, so familiar, brought back memories of happier times.

"I was supposed to meet someone here for lunch," she said, her lips pouting in a way she probably thought was adorable. "But it looks as if I've been stood up. Be a dear and join, me, would you? For old time's sake."

Old time's sake? Was she serious? Benny couldn't help comparing her botoxed, heavily-made-up face to Laura's natural beauty. She reached out and squeezed his hand. "Please? You know how I hate to eat alone."

Benny had every intention of saying no, but something stopped him. Hadn't he wished for someone to love? Was it coincidence that Melody had suddenly showed up in his life again? Or was there more to it? He owed it to himself to find out.

Melody was at her most charming over lunch, laughing in that way she had of throwing back her head and letting loose with a pure burst of pleasure. She reached out and touched the back of his hand, "This is nice, isn't it Benjamin? Like it used to be with us."

He gave a noncommittal sound of agreement.

She gave his hand a squeeze. "I'm sorry Benjamin. I was foolish. I realize that. Can you ever forgive me?"

Could he? Maybe he owed it to both of them to find out. As much as he didn't want to believe it, maybe the box had brought Melody back into his life.

The longer they talked, the more he wanted to believe she'd changed.

She looked around the dining room, giving a nod of approval. Benny saw it through her eyes—the crisp linen tablecloths and glowing votive candles on every table, the fresh flowers in crystal vases. Every little touch added to the elegant ambiance. It was right up Melody's alley. She'd always had expensive tastes. Did that have anything to do with her renewed interest in him?

As soon as she was finished eating, Benny made excuses to escape, but not before Melody suggested they meet one night for dinner. Benny agreed, mostly so he could leave and get back to work. It was a big afternoon at the Country Club.

The conference room had been booked by the Sun Valley Women's Club. They met there once a month and Benny was in charge of the arrangements. Today was a special day, however. After Sally had hinted that Laura's bookstore may be running into financial difficulties, Benny had made a phone call to the president of the Women's Club suggesting they invite Laura to speak, since she was a local small business owner. He'd hoped that the exposure and backing of the Women's Club would increase her visibility in the community and bring in more customers.

They'd agreed and Benny had asked that they not mention it was his suggestion. He was on pins and needles waiting for Laura to arrive. He wanted everything to be perfect.

The room was set up with tables for eight, draped with spotless white tablecloths and the buffet table was ready and waiting for the kitchen staff to set out the food. He'd double checked the microphone at the podium and set up the overhead projector. Everything was in place when the women began arriving.

Benny greeted them all at the door, glancing occasionally at the poster of Laura in front of her bookstore, placed prominently in front of the conference room. The professionally posed head shot couldn't hide the warmth emanating from her eyes, or the curve of her lips as if she was harboring a delightful secret. Approachable yet distant, she was a contradiction. What little Benny knew about her explained her need to keep people at a distance while at the same time she craved intimacy.

Barbara Sullivan, president and organizer of the event, stepped outside and looked right and left, a frown on her face.

"Everything all right?" Benny asked.

"Our speaker hasn't arrived." She glanced at her watch. "We have a few minutes before we're scheduled to start." The concern on her face was evident.

"I'll keep an eye out for her," Benny assured her, guiding the frazzled woman back into the conference room. "You stall the guests and as soon as Laura arrives, I'll usher her inside."

Five minutes later Laura came rushing through the doorway, looking incredible in a clingy red dress that molded to every delectable curve of her body. Benny was glad to see her, not because she was due to speak in a few moments, but because looking at her made him feel happy and warm inside.

He rushed to greet her just as her heel caught on the rug and she tumbled into his outstretched arms. Before either could say a word, they were both startled by the unmistakable sound of ripping fabric. Her eyes widened. "Oh, no!"

Benny made sure she was steady on her feet before releasing her. She stared in horror at the long, gaping side seam of her dress. Her eyes widened, seeming to plead with him to somehow fix this and the look on her face filled him with an overwhelming desire to make things right for her. "Laura…" He took her elbow and guided her toward the small, windowless room that served as his office.

"I'm supposed to be speaking to the Women's Group."

"I know," Benny said. "But we have a few minutes before they get restless in there. Let me help."

Only then did Benny remember the sewing kit that had shown up on his doorstep that morning. He dug it out of the bottom of his briefcase and handed it to her.

She stared blankly at his outstretched hand. "I don't know how to sew," she admitted.

Benny tried hard not to notice the brief flash of skin as she moved. "I can sew it," he said. "But you'll have to take the dress off."

She blinked, then color washed over her cheeks.

Benny reached for the belted trench coat hanging on a hook by the door. He'd worn it to work because they'd predicted rain. And there it hung, as convenient as the sewing kit he'd almost forgotten about in his briefcase. "Put this on," he said, handing it to Laura. "I can have that seam sewn in no time." He turned his back and waited for her to decide.

Moments later, he heard a soft shuffling sound behind him. He tried not to imagine her stripping her dress off in his office, but his imagination had a mind of its own. Then she handed the dress over. He saw only the sleeve of his trench coat over her slim wrist before she pulled away.

"My mother taught me how to sew," he said, trying to ease the uncomfortable situation. He threaded the needle and began to sew the seam in small, even stitches. The fabric was still warm from her body and held the scent of flowers and citrus. It was both enticing and erotic at the same time.

To fill the silence, he chattered as he sewed. "My mother taught all the boys to cook and sew and made sure the girls knew how to change a flat tire or sink a nail. There were no gender roles in our family."

"You're lucky," she said. He heard the wistful yearning in her voice and remembered that she'd grown up wishing for just such a family.

He finished the seam in no time and held the dress to the side. She reached for it, then he heard a soft, swishing sound behind him and imagined the fabric falling over her body. Would she feel the heat of his hands along her skin? Would she sense his longing?

"Perfect," she said. "How can I thank you?"

He turned and saw her slide her hands down the front of her dress, releasing any wrinkles that might have been left behind. Then she fluffed her hair.

"No thanks necessary." He checked his watch. "Two minutes to spare."

With that she was off and running for her presentation. After she left, Benny could have kicked himself. Why hadn't he said she could repay him by going out to dinner? Oh yeah, because she was engaged.

Which made him think of Melody. She'd broken his heart once and she was back looking for forgiveness. But how do you forgive someone who'd lied and cheated as she had? The pain of betrayal still weighed on his heart. He'd sworn then he'd never let another woman make a fool of him again.

Pushing thoughts of Melody aside, Benny slipped into the conference room to hear Laura speak. Her presentation was about adapting to a changing marketplace. All traces of the anxious woman who'd entered earlier were gone. Laura spoke with confidence, her voice clear and strong. At that moment he fell a little bit in love with her.

Melody and Laura. There was no comparison. If he believed in the power of the magic box, then hadn't today proved that Laura was the answer to his wish? Hadn't the sewing kit turned up on his doorstep right after he'd wished for someone to love? And the sewing kit had come to Laura's rescue after she'd fallen right into his arms. All evidence pointed to her being the one.

Except Laura was engaged. So much for magic. He turned and closed the door, all of his hopes and dreams dashed in an instant. Returning to his office, Benny tossed the sewing kit into the waste basket.

****

Laura arrived home, fresh from a successful presentation with the Women's Business Group. Not only had they promised to help her with marketing and promotion, but they'd offered her a grant that would keep her afloat for the next few months.

Ivy had offered to cover the bookstore for the rest of the afternoon. Not that there were a lot of customers these days. With the afternoon off, Laura decided to go for a walk. The sun was bright in the sky, chasing the chill from the air. It felt wonderful to walk in the sunshine. She straightened her shoulders, feeling as if a weight had been lifted. Even though it was only a temporary reprieve, it would give her time to come up with more strategies to build her business into something bigger and stronger.

She reached the park and noticed children on the playground. The sound of their laughter wrenched her heart. Lately she'd been fighting the urge to have a child of her own, but the timing wasn't right. Oh, it wasn't because she didn't have a man in her life right now. That could be easily rectified. She could always adopt, if not from Hyatt House, then another agency whose rules and regulations weren't as stringent. And she had no problem being a single mother. But not yet. Not until her store was solvent and she knew she could provide for a child's every need.

Gabe's face came to mind. Yes, a little boy exactly like Gabe would be perfect. Or a little girl, all pretty in pink, who she could shower with fashion dolls and ballet slippers and all the things she herself had wished for growing up.

She sat on a bench by a small pond and let the rippling waters soothe her soul. After a few minutes someone came up and sat beside her. She glanced over and saw Nick, his beard pulled tight with a rubber band and a red bandana covering his white hair. He looked less like Santa and more like Santa's bad-ass brother.

"I thought that was you sitting here," he said. "Who's watching the store?"

"Ivy's covering. I had a presentation with the Women's Group today at the Country Club. It went very well and they offered me a grant which will keep the creditors at bay for a few months."

"That's great," Nick said. "Did you run into our friend Benjamin?"

Laura nodded. "Yes, as a matter of fact, I did. Funny story. I slipped and tore my dress. It just so happened he had a sewing kit handy and came to my rescue."

Nick nodded. "Hmmm…"

There seemed to be a lot unsaid in that single sound. She frowned. "You don't think Benny had anything to do with me getting that grant, do you?"

Nick shrugged. "I don't know. Just wondering,

that's all." He winked at Laura and stood. "You need a ride home?"

She glanced at the motorcycle parked beside the bench. "On your Harley?"

He leaned close. "It's called a Hog, honey."

Laura stood up and shook her head. "No thanks, I'm enjoying this nice weather. You and your hog get home safe."

"I will," he said. "Oh, and Beverley says to come over for dinner one of these nights. She wants to try out some of those new recipes and we get to be her guinea pigs."

"I'll give her a call," Laura said. "The thought of one of Beverley's home-cooked meals made her realize how hungry she was. Maybe a trip to Sonny's Diner was in order to celebrate her successful presentation today with their famous meatloaf and buttermilk biscuits.

She waved goodbye to Nick and headed in the other direction toward her favorite diner and a warm meal.

****

Melody was at her most charming. She'd ordered an expensive bottle of wine with dinner. Benny didn't mind. He could afford the best, and the best is what Melody had always expected. He wondered if she'd have stuck by him when he'd lost his job and couldn't give her the finer things in life. Would she have left him for another man? Again? Was she even now playing him for a fool?

Benny tried to push those thoughts out of his mind. He owed it to her to try to put the past behind them and give it another try.

"So how long have you been working at the country club?"

"Since the beginning of the year." He sliced into his steak. It was cooked to perfection, but he'd lost his appetite. And Melody had lost her appeal. It wasn't even that he couldn't forgive her. He had. But he couldn't concentrate on anything Melody was saying.

All he could think of was the woman who'd fallen into his arms—the smattering of freckles across peach skin, the fall of silky hair, chestnut that shimmered with red and gold highlights. And her eyes. He could have stared into them forever.

Could it be that the love of his life had dropped right into his arms? And what good would it do to find her if he couldn't have her in the end?

That was the question he asked Mrs. Sobieski over coffee and donuts the next morning. It was their usual Saturday morning treat.

"You know," she said, cutting her regular maple-glazed donut into four equal-sized quarters. "I almost didn't marry Oliver." Her eyes gazed into the distance as if she was staring into the past.

Benny leaned forward, chin resting on his palm. "I wish I'd met him."

"Oh, you would have loved Ollie." Her smile brightened. "Never met a person he didn't like. And, to be honest, there wasn't anyone who didn't like him. Sometimes I was a little jealous of the way people tripped over each other to be his friend."

"Sounds like a great guy."

Sally nodded. "He was. But I didn't trust it at first. I didn't think anyone could be that nice, that polite, that well liked. I thought it had to be an act."

Benny nodded. He knew Sally well enough by now to realize she could be a little cynical.

"So, when he proposed the first time…"

"The first time? How many times did he have to propose?"

She shrugged. "Three. Or four. I don't remember exactly." The coquettish smile on her face made her look like a love-struck teenager again. "The thing is, I didn't think I was ready. I didn't think he was sincere. Oh, I had a million and one reasons to say no."

"But?"

"There was one reason to say yes," she said. "I was crazy about him."

Benny could easily imagine Sally as a young, love-struck girl. "How long were you married?"

"We were married thirty-five years. We had our ups and downs. Every marriage does. If you have more ups than downs, it's a good marriage." She grinned. "We had a good marriage." She frowned, plopped a piece of donut into her mouth and chewed with a thoughtful expression on her face. She turned to Benny, her eyes shimmering. "Not marrying him would have been the biggest mistake of my life."

He reached out and placed his hand over hers.

She blinked back tears. "I wouldn't trade those years for anything. But what I'm trying to say is don't give up. What if Ollie had given up the first time I said no? But he didn't. He came back and showed me why we were right for each other every single time. Perseverance wins the prize."

"That's different," Benny said, picking up the check. "You weren't engaged to another man."

"Funny about that," Sally said. "I've never seen

Laura with another man. She never talks about her fiancé or has pictures of him anywhere."

Benny shrugged. That didn't mean anything. "I was almost married once," he said.

At Sally's questioning glance, he continued. "Her name was Melody. We were young, I thought I knew her, but it turned out I didn't. She'd been lying to me all along. Seeing another man." Benny shook his head. "Luckily I found out before going through with the wedding."

"It wasn't meant to be," Sally said.

Maybe. But Benny felt the sting of loss and betrayal over again. "Funny thing," he said. "She turned up again. Wanted me to give her a second chance."

"And?"

"I forgave her," he said. "But you can't build a future on lies. I knew I could never trust her again. Or any other woman for that matter."

"Oh Benny," Sally patted his wrist. "Not every woman will break your heart. Somewhere out there is a woman who will treasure your love and give it back to you in return."

Despite the wish he'd made, Benny had a hard time believing that.

****

Benny was only fifteen minutes early getting to the office the following Monday, as opposed to his usual habit of getting in half an hour early, which was why Coralee was already at the front desk when he arrived.

"Got a secret admirer?" she asked.

Benny stared at her with a blank expression.

She jerked her head to the side, and he followed her gaze to a vase of daisies on the counter. "For me?"

"Seems that way." Her smile was both amused and curious. "You're the only Benny here, as far as I know."

He checked the envelope that came with the flowers. Sure enough, his name was written across the front. Tearing it open, he read the card inside. *Thank you for coming to my rescue.* It was signed Laura, with a flourish and a little heart at the end.

The heart was cute, but he probably shouldn't read anything into it. Most likely she signed her name that way all the time. He tucked the card into his pocket just the same, then carried the vase into his office. Suddenly daisies were his favorite flower.

Benny went about his day only half paying attention to his duties. Thoughts of Laura distracted him—the way she smelled, the smoky gray of her eyes, the way she'd felt in his arms. Every time he glanced at the daisies on his desk, he thought of her and smiled.

Wasn't it just like him to fall for a woman who was unavailable?

The thought of going on another blind date held no appeal. If nothing else, this proved the box held no magic after all.

Chapter Eleven

Benny loved summer. There was so much to do at the country club, between making sure the greens and pool were maintained properly and seeing to the needs of their guests, his days were full, and he loved every minute of it.

On his way past the Country Club Cafe, he spotted Sally sitting at an outdoor table, dressed in a brightly colored lounging dress and a straw hat. She waved to him and he wandered over.

"Surprise!" she cried out.

Only then did he notice the small birthday cake, big enough for two, and the table set with plates and silverware. He took the other seat, touched beyond words at her gesture. "How did you know it was my birthday?"

"I have my ways," she said, then reached in her tote bag and pulled out a wrapped gift. "Happy birthday, Benny."

He shook his head. "You shouldn't have."

"I wanted to," she said. "You've done so much for me. You're like another son." She made a shooing gesture. "Now open it."

He did and felt tears sting his eyes when he saw the title of the book in his hand—*The Scent of Moonlight*, by Hester Carter, his paternal grandmother. "I can't believe you found it."

"Well. I can't take all the credit. Laura at the bookstore tracked it down for me. It came in last week. Just in the nick of time."

He stood and walked around the table to give Sally a warm hug. "Thank you so much. I think this is one of the nicest things anyone has ever done for me."

"I couldn't help but read through some of the poems before wrapping the book. They're very good. You should be proud."

Benny returned to his seat and thumbed through the book. Sally was right. They were beautiful and evocative. He wished he'd gotten to know this woman, but she'd died when he was a baby. As the youngest of four, he had fewer memories of relatives than some of his older siblings, which made this gift even more poignant.

There was a picture of his grandmother on the back cover. She was plain, with a long nose and tightly curled hair, but her smile was the kind of smile that drew people in and made them want to sit at her knee while she told long, heartwarming stories.

He clutched the book to his chest. He couldn't wait to show it to his family. He'd been saving up for airline tickets, hoping everyone could be together for Thanksgiving. So far, half of his siblings planned to make it, but the rest were still up in the air.

After sharing cake with Sally, he finished the afternoon with a smile on his face. Every time he glanced at the book on his desk, he was overcome with a sense of family connection. He was grateful and wanted to thank Laura for her part in finding the book. Not sure whether the bookstore would be open or not, he took a chance and stopped by on his way home.

When he saw the store was open, his heart stuttered, and when he stepped inside and saw Laura setting up a Fourth of July display, it seemed to leap in his chest. Her hair was down today, flowing partway down her back in thick waves. He imagined what it would feel like to brush a wayward tendril from her face, or to run his fingers through those lush waves.

She turned and when she saw him a smile lit up her face. "Benny, it's so nice to see you."

He closed the distance between them and held out the book. "I wanted to come by and thank you for helping Sally track down this book. It means the world to me."

"You're very welcome," she said. "I glanced through it. Your grandmother was a very talented writer. I couldn't find any other books, though. I wonder if she stopped writing after this one."

"From what I understand, she died young. I never knew her, which is why this book means so much to me." He turned the book over, looking at her picture.

"You have her eyes," Laura said, taking the book from his hands to study the picture. "And her smile."

"Have you ever imagined seeing yourself in someone else's features," he asked.

"Yes," was all she said. That was one of the hardest parts of not having a family history. There was no one who looked like her, thought the way she did, or shared the same talents. Laura gestured to the coffee bar. "Can I buy you a cup of coffee?"

He nodded. "That would be great."

Ivy poured them each a cup, then looked from one to the other. "I think I'm going to head out a little early if that's okay."

"No problem," Laura said. "I'll close up."

Benny gestured to the display. "Hard to believe it's almost July. The Fourth of July was always a big day for our family. Every year we had a big family picnic with cookouts, volleyball games, and swimming in the pool. Grown-ups, kids, new babies—everyone came together for a day of fun."

That old, familiar yearning crept up on her. A yearning for home and family that still haunted her despite the progress she'd made since leaving Hyatt House a dozen years ago at the tender age of eighteen.

"You miss them," she said.

"I do. But I'm trying to arrange a family reunion for Thanksgiving. My brother's house in Texas is probably more centrally located for everyone and since he has the hardest time getting away from work, he suggested we meet there."

Laura glanced down at her coffee. "Sounds like fun," she murmured.

"If we can get everyone there," he said. "Right now, it's about fifty percent. But my mom and dad have agreed to fly in. We're all pitching in to buy them tickets."

"Sounds like you had the perfect family life."

He chuckled. "We had our ups and downs, like most families. I was the youngest, so I always felt I didn't measure up. My brothers were over achievers, and I was just…normal, I guess. I didn't play football or soccer, wasn't valedictorian of my class, and didn't end up with a brilliant career as a doctor or lawyer. I felt alone, like I was the only one without big goals and dreams."

He stopped and frowned. "It didn't help when I lost my job last year."

Laura was surprised to hear that someone growing up in a big, close-knit family could still feel alone. She'd assumed that people who had family around them never felt alone or insecure.

"Sometimes I felt like I was a disappointment to my family."

"I'm sure that's not the case." She may have thought that six months ago when she first saw him at the community center, but not now. She'd seen the pride he took in his job and how caring he was. "Hey, if not for you, I would have had to give my speech to the Women's Group with a torn dress."

He laughed along with her. "You were brilliant," A flush of color spread across his cheeks. "I heard some of your speech," he admitted. "It was good."

"Thanks. And because of that, they awarded me a grant and advertised my business through their networking channels. It's been great for business. I have you to thank."

"You did it all on your own," he said. "This is a great store. It's warm and welcoming, like being in someone's living room. The only thing missing is a cat curled up in a shaft of sunlight to make the picture complete."

Laura laughed and shook her head. "No pets for me. Pets equal commitment."

Benny gave her a questioning look. "Everything is a commitment. Having a child, buying a house, or..." he gestured to take in the bookstore, "...starting your own business. Life is a commitment."

Laura didn't bother contradicting him. He had a

lifetime worth of honored commitments to rely on. She didn't. The only person who'd even tried to make a commitment to her was Edna Hyatt, and sickness had forced her to break that promise. As far as Laura was concerned, committing to something or someone was merely another road leading to disappointment and heartbreak.

Laura noticed Benny staring at the ring she'd moved to her opposite hand. He glanced up. "I, uh, noticed you're not wearing your engagement ring, um...I mean." He seemed at a loss for words. "Is everything okay?"

"Sure, why?"

"I just thought you were engaged, and now..."

"Oh." Laura twisted the ring. "No, this was a gift from Edna Hyatt, the founder of Hyatt House. She gave it to me as a reminder..." Laura wasn't sure how much she wanted to share. As much as she wanted to confide in Benny, she wasn't ready to completely drop her guard.

"So, you weren't engaged?"

"No."

Benny gave an understanding nod. "It makes a nice shield to keep people away."

He was more observant than she'd given him credit for. Before she could respond, he asked. "What changed?"

That was a good question. Was it something Edna had said? Or was it the way she'd felt falling into Benny's arms. Safe. Secure. Maybe for the first time in her life she trusted someone to catch her when she fell.

"Hey," Benny said, interrupting her train of thought. "Have you had dinner yet?" He stopped and stuttered. "I'm uh, I'm sure you already have plans."

"I'd like that," she said, surprising herself. After all, it was only dinner, not a commitment.

They walked the few blocks to one of her favorite restaurants. "I hope you like Indian food," she said.

"Honestly?" He grinned sheepishly. "I've never tried it. I'm more of a meat and potatoes kind of guy."

"Well, we'll change that," she said.

Benny liked the way that sounded. Especially the *we* part. It sounded like a promise of dinners to come.

Stepping inside, Benny was met with an assortment of colors, smells, and textures. He took a deep breath, inhaling the pungent aroma of turmeric and smoky cumin, as well as hint of cinnamon and ginger. Moroccan archways separated intimate seating corners, all splashed with bright reds and golds. The walls were decorated with intricately carved mandalas and vibrant prints. Benny felt as if he'd been transported to another time and place.

When they were seated, Laura started ordering dishes he'd never heard of—reshami kabab, murg tikka masala, tandoori roasted chicken with basmati rice and tandoori naan, along with spicy masala chai tea.

"How many people are we feeding?" he asked.

She smiled. "I want you to have a variety of things to try. I'm sure you'll find a favorite among these dishes. Besides, what we don't eat we can take home to warm up tomorrow night."

He trusted her judgment, and when the food came, he wasn't disappointed. "Oh my God, how have I gone so long without eating this heavenly food?"

"That's a good question. What else have you missed, Mr. Meat and Potatoes?"

Linda Bleser

He folded a piece of Naan bread, dipped it in the heavenly butter sauce and popped it into his mouth. He chewed with slow appreciation before answering. "I don't know, but I'd be happy to have you introduce me to more."

Maybe it was the candlelight, but her eyes seemed to sparkle. Benny knew he was a goner. "You should start a food blog," he said.

She seemed to mull the idea over. "Not a bad idea. I do love trying new foods and visiting local restaurants. Food never disappoints."

She looked away, as if she'd said too much. His heart broke for her and he wanted to take her in his arms and assure her that he'd never leave or disappoint her. But it was way too soon to make those kinds of grand statements. She was too guarded. He'd have to chip away at that armor a tiny piece at a time.

He realized he was jumping ahead far too quickly. Although he was relieved to know she wasn't engaged, he still wasn't convinced that someone like her could fall for a guy like him. Now that he knew she was available, he could at least try to win her heart.

He heard Nick's voice in his head. *Trust the box.* Hadn't the box provided the very thing that he'd needed when she'd fallen into his arms?

And it wasn't as if he was that out-of-work guy she'd met a year ago. He had a job. A good job with pay raises and promotions. And enough money saved so he could afford a down payment on a house with a nice yard where they could raise a bunch of kids.

Maybe even Gabe.

It was only June, but Benny already knew what his next wish was going to be. He wanted a home and a family, the white picket fence, kids playing in the yard, and a wife who was a partner, friend, and lover. He wanted it all. Laura had that effect on him. She made him want to be a better man, to do better things, and to be able to offer her everything she'd been denied all of her life. He wanted to give her the world.

After they finished their meal, Benny walked Laura back to her apartment, which was a studio loft above the bookstore. "That's convenient," Benny said when she told him. "Now I'll know where to find you."

He had a moment of regret. Did that make him sound like a stalker?

She simply smiled. "Only if you plan on going out for something other than meat and potatoes."

"I'm looking forward to it."

"On one condition," she said. "Next time I pick up the check." She held up her hand before he could argue. "Yes or no?"

Afraid that saying no would mean the end of their dinner dates, he gave a sheepish yes. "Next Friday? Same time?"

"Okay."

Her smile brightened her entire face and Benny couldn't help smiling back. She bounced up on her toes and gave him a quick peck on the cheek before turning to go inside. After the door closed, Benny stood there for several minutes, stunned by this turn of events.

Trust the box.

Could it be that simple?

As soon as he arrived home, Benny called the florist and ordered a dozen daisies to be delivered to the bookstore in the morning.

Chapter Twelve

The screech of brakes and squeal of tires woke Benny from a sound sleep. He sat straight up in bed, blinking the sleep from his eyes. He'd almost convinced himself the sound was leftover remnants of a dream, when he heard a pitiful wail outside his window. He scurried out of bed, slipped on a pair of pants, and opened his door at the same time that Sally threw her door open.

"What was that?" she asked, tying a belt around a pink housecoat.

"Not sure," Benny said. "I'll go check."

He opened the outside door to see a tiny ball of fur limping across the sidewalk. It was yellow and white, and looked exactly like the cat he'd had as a young boy. Goldie had been the best cat ever, coming into his life as a tiny kitten when Benny was six. They'd grown up together. Goldie had passed quietly in her sleep when Benny was away at college. He'd always felt guilty that he hadn't been there to soothe and comfort her in the end.

This kitten limped toward Benny, looked up at him with pitiful eyes, and let loose a tiny mew.

"Oh, you poor thing. You wait right here," he said, gently stroking the cat. "I'll be right back."

Benny rushed into his apartment and grabbed a soft

towel. The cat was curled up on the doorstep when he returned. He gently wrapped it in the towel, talking gently and soothingly as he carried it inside.

"Oh, the poor thing," Sally cried. "Is he okay?"

"I think he's hurt," Benny said. A pitiful mewl confirmed his assessment.

He handed the kitten over to Sally, then poured some milk into a bowl and placed it on the floor. When Sally eased the kitten down in front of the bowl, it simply stared, then backed away. The look it gave Benny broke his heart. The kitten was thin and scrawny. Who knew when he had last eaten? Apparently, the injuries were more pressing than food, Benny guessed.

"I have to take him to the vet," Benny said.

"I'll go with you," Sally said. "Just let me get changed. I'll only be a minute."

While he waited, Benny looked up the address of a 24-hour emergency veterinarian. He called ahead to make sure someone would be available, then finished dressing in time for Sally to emerge from her apartment.

She held the kitten while Benny drove the ten minutes to the veterinarian. Benny glanced over to see the kitten curled up in her arms, its tiny tongue rasping against the curve of her hand. "He likes you."

"Or she." Sally cooed to the trembling animal. "It's okay, sweetie. We're going to take real good care of you." Then she frowned. "We're not allowed to have pets in the apartment, you know."

"Yeah. Well, we'll cross that bridge when we come to it. Who knows, this little guy—or girl—may belong to someone who's searching all over. Maybe it has one of those chips or something to find its owner."

As it turned out, the kitten didn't have a chip. "Most likely left by the side of the road," the vet said. "Happens all the time."

"I think it was hit by a car," Benny said. "I heard tires screeching, then a howl of pain.

The vet manipulated the kitten's leg. The cat hissed and pulled away, then, as if apologizing for its reaction, licked the vet's finger. "Let's take a few x-rays," he said. "Just to be sure. But I don't think there are any broken bones."

Benny returned to the waiting room where Sally was in deep conversation with another woman. Benny smiled to himself. That's the way Sally was. Leave her alone with someone for five minutes and she'd have their whole life history in a nutshell.

"Oh Benny, there you are. This is Opal Grainger. She lives just outside of River's Bend. She's thinking of moving to Florida," Sally said. "I was telling her your parents moved to Florida and maybe you could give her some advice on that."

"Sure." Benny took a seat beside them. "My parents are living in a retirement community and they love it. They said it's like day camp for adults—clubs, swimming pools, sports activities and entertainment. They're always on the go."

"Sounds lovely," Opal said. "Did they buy a house, or do they rent?"

"Actually, they're living in a condo right now. They said there's less upkeep and commitment. Do you have a house here?"

"Yes, an old farmhouse on three acres."

Having grown up in the city, Benny had no concept

of what three acres looked like, but it sounded like a lot of property.

The woman continued. "Raised our kids there. Lots of room for the dogs to run, and a garden in the back. But it's getting to be too much for us to keep up. We're getting old and the thought of retiring to Florida sounds better and better all the time."

Suddenly Benny flashed back on his conversation with Laura about commitment—a house, a child, a marriage. He was ready for all those things. Isn't that what he'd decided to wish for? A place to call home and someday raise a family?

"This is going to sound strange," he said. "But would you mind if I looked at the house before you put it on the market? I'd like to start a family one day, and your house sounds perfect."

Sally cocked her head, but didn't interrupt, even though Benny could see her mind was swirling with questions.

"Oh, it is," Opal replied. "There's a fireplace to hang Christmas stockings, a big dining room for a growing family, and lots of yard to play in."

Benny gave her his card. "Call me if you decide to sell." Something told him he'd be hearing from her, and the house would be exactly what he would have wished for. He still wasn't ready to believe in magic, but wasn't it a coincidence that an injured kitten on his doorstep had led him straight to someone selling a house big enough to raise a family?

The receptionist called Benny into the doctor's office, interrupting his thoughts. "She's going to be fine," the doctor told him. "A few scrapes and sprains, but nothing is broken. She should be good as new in a few weeks."

Benny picked up the kitten, who curled up against his neck. "She?"

"Yes, she's a girl. What are you going to name her?"

Benny didn't have to think long. "Daisy," he said, petting the yellow and white kitten until he heard her purr against his ear.

"Stop at the desk and make an appointment to bring Daisy in for her shots in a week or so and we'll see how she's doing, but I'm guessing she'll be up and running before then."

Benny shook the doctor's hand. "Thank you."

On his way out, he nodded to Mrs. Grainger, who smiled in return. Yes, it was all going to work out. Benny was sure of it.

Sally glanced at her watch. "Oh Benny, you're going to be late for work."

He shook his head. "I called in before we left. I have the morning off. And I have a good idea what I'm going to do."

He confided his plans to Sally and she agreed wholeheartedly to help him pull it off.

Their first stop was the pet store where Benny stocked up on cat toys, cat food, and a soft cushioned bed for Daisy to sleep in. He splurged on a pet carrier as well. Twenty minutes later he and his accomplice were back on the road, Daisy sleeping peacefully in her car carrier.

"Do you think she'll agree?"

Benny took a deep breath and let it out with a sigh. "I sure hope so."

They arrived at the bookstore just as Laura was

opening for the day. "What a nice surprise," she said, greeting them at the door.

"I've come to ask you a favor," Benny said. "There was an accident outside our apartment this morning."

"Oh!" Laura looked from one to the other with alarm. "Is everyone okay?"

"Yes, but there was an injury." He held up the carrier where Daisy rubbed the side of her head against the opening, then licked her front paw. "We brought her to the vet, and he said she'll heal up in no time, but..." he glanced at Sally, who nodded her head and finished for him.

"We can't have pets at the apartment," she said. "The landlord will kick us out if he finds her there."

Laura blinked, as understanding dawned in her eyes. "No, I don't think..."

"Please," Sally begged. "There's nowhere else for her to go. She's so sweet and won't be any trouble at all. And Benny bought everything you need to keep her happy until he can buy a place of his own where he can have all the pets he wants." She glanced at Benny. "Right?"

It was like watching a tennis match, Laura thought, turning from one to the other.

"Give it a few days," Benny said. "Then if you decide it's not going to work out, we'll take her to the shelter."

"Where they'll probably put the poor little thing to sleep," Sally said with a woeful grimace.

Oh, now she wasn't playing fair. Laura wiggled her finger in the front of the carrier and the kitten batted it playfully. "She is kind of cute."

"She's adorable," Sally said. "And she won't be

any trouble. I bet she'd be a good mouser. Every bookstore needs a good mouser."

"What's her name?"

It was Benny who replied. "Daisy."

That was it—the final word that broke down all of her resolve. She opened the cage and cradled the yellow and white striped kitten. "Daisy, huh?"

Benny shrugged. "Seemed appropriate."

Laura held his gaze for a long moment, then glanced at the shopping bags at his feet. "Let's see what you've got there."

****

Benny half expected Laura to call during the week and insist he take the cat back. He was afraid to stop in the bookstore in case she'd decided Daisy was too much of a commitment. So far, so good.

He woke up early Sunday morning craving pancakes. He made his way to a small neighborhood diner only a few blocks away. Sonny's had the best short-order cook in town and their menu consisted of mouth-watering comfort food—the kind his mother used to make.

The smell of bacon teased his senses as soon as he opened the door. Inside the scents were layered with undertones of sugar, butter and cinnamon, convincing him he'd made the right choice.

The hostess ushered him to a table, but Benny stopped when he spotted a familiar face at a corner booth. "Laura?"

She looked up from her eBook reader and smiled. "Benny. Hi!" Her smile was sincere, as was her voice when she asked if he'd like to join her.

"Absolutely," he said, taking a seat beside her.

"Have you ordered yet?"

"Just coffee."

Benny did the same, then turned to the menu. Laura's menu remained closed beside her. "This isn't your usual dining experience," he said. "It's not exotic, just good old American fare."

She nodded, then looked down and fiddled with her spoon. Then, as if coming to a decision, she looked Benny in the eye. "I told you I grew up in Hyatt House, right?"

"Yes."

"Well, every day of the week we either had cold cereal or oatmeal for breakfast. But on Sunday..." she took a deep breath and let it out slowly. "Sunday, we had fresh eggs that Nick delivered the night before."

When the waitress stopped by, Benny ordered a cup of coffee and told her they weren't ready to order yet.

"So, Nick would bring eggs on Saturday," he said, encouraging her to continue her story.

"Yes, and on Sundays we had eggs for breakfast—scrambled eggs, poached eggs, or fried eggs with toast triangles dipped in runny yellow yolks." Her eyes went distant, as if reliving those Sunday mornings. "To this day," she said, "I associate Sunday morning with eggs."

What she didn't tell him was that it was a tradition she continued to this day. Probably the only tradition she could call her own. Most days she'd grab a yogurt or toast before rushing off to work, but on Sunday she treated herself to a full-blown breakfast that always included eggs.

Benny had been watching Laura's face. She probably didn't realize how expressive her face was.

While she kept her tone even, every emotion she felt was evident on her face, and for a brief moment he glimpsed that little girl who was grateful for something as simple as eggs for breakfast, something he'd taken for granted all his life.

The waitress stopped by the table with their coffee and asked if they were ready to order. Laura ordered a cheese omelet, turkey bacon and a fruit cup. "I'll have the same," Benny said, all thoughts of pancakes forgotten. "Except I'll have home fries instead of fruit."

When the waitress walked away, Benny reached out and put his hand over Laura's. "Thank you for sharing your memories with me," he said. "It couldn't have been easy."

Laura shook her head from side to side. "Somehow you make it easy to share." She was quiet for a moment, as if trying to figure out a riddle. The silence was comfortable, however.

"Nick's wife Beverley. She was the cook at Hyatt House? And now she owns the bakery and makes fruitcakes."

"Well, she makes more than fruitcakes. Her rum cake is out of this world. She's the one who taught me to bake, you know."

Benny shook his head. "I didn't know. You're full of surprises."

Just then, their food arrived, and Laura dug into her breakfast as if she was afraid someone would take it away. It was another minor glimpse at the little girl who'd had to claw and scratch for her share. Benny was overcome with a desire to make sure she never wanted for anything again.

"So," he said as they finished up their breakfasts.

"You said Nick's wife Beverley taught you to bake?"

"Yes, I worked in her bakery part-time when I was a teenager. She taught me everything she knows about baking. I can make cookies and cakes, pies and tarts, breads, muffins and biscuits that will melt in your mouth."

"Mmmm…will you marry me?"

Laura blinked her eyes and stared. Benny realized he'd put his foot in his mouth. "I was just kidding," he said. "Not that I don't…I mean, you know, the way to a man's heart and all."

With a wave of her hand, she put him at ease. "It's okay. I understand."

Did she, though? What if he told her that she could be the answer to his wish for someone to love? No, too soon. Instead he asked her if they were still on for dinner Friday.

"Yes," she said. "I'll pick you up at six o'clock. Come hungry."

"No clues to where we're going?"

"Nope, it's a surprise."

Benny was up for a surprise. As long as it meant spending time with Laura, he was up for anything.

****

The following Friday Laura picked Benny up at his apartment. He met her outside, anxious to find out where they were going next.

"Have you lived here long?" she asked, gesturing toward the apartment complex.

"It's temporary," he told her. "I've been saving up for a down payment on a house, but I don't want to leave Sally alone here right now. She's in the apartment across the hall."

"She thinks the world of you."

"Oh?" Benny was secretly proud that Sally had mentioned him.

"I overheard her talking to Ivy. She said you've been a big help to her since her husband died."

"Ollie," Benny said. "I never met him, but he sounds like a great guy. I know Sally misses him terribly. I don't think she's adjusted to being alone, so she's comfortable knowing I'm right across the hall if she needs anything."

Laura gave him an approving look but didn't comment. A few minutes later she parked in front of a restaurant called the Acropolis. Greek columns decorated the outside. The inside was cool white, and blues that rivaled the sea. Frescoes covered the walls, vibrating with energy.

As usual, Benny let Laura order for him. They started with saganaki, a flaming cheese dish heralded with enthusiastic shouts of "Opa!" Next came dishes of spanakopita and souvlaki. Between courses they were treated to a variety of experiences, from plate breaking to napkin throwing to Zorba dancing. An exotic belly dancer with long, dark hair worked her way through the crowd, eliciting cheers from the diners, who tucked tips into her hip scarf. There was an air of excitement to the meal that Benny had never experienced before. He felt as if he'd taken a crash course in Greek culture.

They toasted with ouzo and afterward Benny reached out and took Laura's hand, delighted when she didn't pull away.

"This is fun," he said. "Can I choose next?"

"As long as it's something you haven't tried before, that's fine with me. I'm trying to expand your food horizons."

"I'm not complaining," he squeezed her hand. "You're doing a fabulous job. But I want to discover new dining experiences too."

"Ah, so you're enjoying the thrill of the chase. That's exactly what I'd hoped for."

"How did you become such a foodie?"

"When I was young, I read about all these exotic dishes in books, but our meals at the shelter were pretty basic—macaroni and cheese, peanut butter and jelly sandwiches, and meatloaf were some of our staples. I vowed that when I grew up, I'd try all the exotic dishes I'd read about in my books. Extra points if it's an immersive experience so I feel as if I've traveled to another country."

She grinned. "I may not be able to physically travel to exotic countries, but I can eat my way around the world without ever leaving home."

Benny felt as if she'd opened a secret doorway, allowing him to see a part of herself she kept hidden from the rest of the world. "Thank you," he said.

"For?"

"For allowing me to join you on your around-the-world food tour."

They lingered over drinks, enjoying the atmosphere and each other's company. This time when they said good night, Benny pulled her into his arms for a long, lingering kiss.

She leaned into him, her body molding to his. He wrapped one arm around her, pulling her close and with the other he reached up to cup the side of her face. His heartbeat thrummed so hard he was sure she could feel it pounding between them. The world stilled for a moment and the only thing that mattered was the way she felt in his arms, the smell of her sweet perfume, and the taste of her on his lips.

In that moment, he knew his prayer had been answered. He'd found the love of his life, with or without the help of Nick's magic box.

****

When she returned home, Laura fairly glided upstairs to her apartment. What was happening to her? She hadn't expected to fall in love, but somehow Benny had inched his way into her heart and now she found herself thinking about him during the day, waiting for his calls, and looking forward to their dinner dates.

A part of her held back, however. The part that expected people to leave her. That voice was louder in the quiet of the evening when doubt reared its ugly head and cautioned her not to trust anyone with her happiness.

Daisy greeted her at the door, weaving between her legs and rubbing the side of her head against each ankle. Laura reached down and scooped the kitten up, burying her face in the soft kitty fur. "How's my girl today? Did you miss me?"

Laura would have sworn she'd never be one of those people who had one-sided conversations with animals. Then again, she'd never thought she'd own a pet. But here she was, in love with a ball of yellow fur.

Thanks to Benny, who seemed to anticipate her every need.

She opened a can of cat food claiming to be gourmet something or other and spooned it into Daisy's dish, then turned on her laptop. She scrolled through her email and opened a message from Carol. It was short and to the point. —*Gabe is back at the shelter. The foster family didn't work out.*—

"Oh no," she murmured. She knew exactly how he felt. She wanted to rush over there and hold him in her arms and tell him everything would be all right. Maybe part of her wanted to say the same to her inner child. She glanced at the clock, already knowing it was too late. The kids would all be in bed.

First thing in the morning, though, she intended to be there. She scratched Daisy behind the ear. "What do you think, girl? Want to come with me and play with some of the kids. Bet they'd love you."

The kitten purred, as if agreeing to the idea.

Chapter Thirteen

Leaving Ivy to cover the bookstore the next morning, Laura packed Daisy in her carrier and went to the shelter. Carol had gathered the children in the playroom, promising them a special surprise. When Laura let Daisy out, they gathered around, ooing and aahing over the kitten.

Laura sat on the floor with the circle of children. "You have to be careful with her," she cautioned them. "She has some injuries that are healing, but if you're too rough it'll hurt her."

As if to make a liar out of her, Daisy went from one lap to the next, climbing up to lick faces and rub her cheek on each of the children. "I think she'd make a great therapy pet," Carol said, watching the cat give equal attention to each boy and girl. "When did you adopt her?"

"I didn't have much choice," Laura replied. "Benny rescued her and can't have a cat in his apartment. He thought she'd make a great addition to the bookstore."

"He's right. Every bookstore should have a resident cat."

"Hmm...I wasn't convinced. But I've grown attached to her."

"And Benny?"

Laura smiled. "Benny rescued me when I was supposed to speak to the women's group."

Carol tilted her head and gave Laura a questioning look. "How so?"

"Oh, I tripped and fell. You know what a klutz I can be. I tore the seam out of my dress right before I was supposed to go on stage."

"Wow, so how did Benny come to your rescue?"

"Turns out the man can sew and even had a sewing kit in his briefcase. He fixed that seam in no time and I was able to make my presentation without a hitch."

"I guess he's a born rescuer."

Laura smiled at the memory. "I sent him daisies to thank him."

"Ah," Carol said, glancing at the kitten. "Her name makes sense now." She gave Laura a knowing glance. "Have you given any more thought to my idea?"

"About a marriage of convenience?" Laura shook her head. "No. Absolutely not. When I get married, it will be for all the right reasons, not based on a lie."

Carol held up her hand. "Okay, just checking."

Gabe toddled over to Laura and plopped onto her lap. "Can she stay here?"

"No," Laura said. "She's going home with me."

She saw the sadness in his eyes even before he whispered. "She's a lucky cat."

Those simple words went straight to Laura's heart. "We're not leaving yet," Laura assured the boy. "You can play with Daisy for a little while more."

Laura spent the better part of the day with the children. They all seemed happier after interacting with the kitten. She felt as if Daisy had healed something in each of them and when she went home, Laura realized a long-sheltered part of her was healing as well.

****

That evening Benny surprised her with dinner at a Brazilian Steakhouse. "What do you think?" he asked when they were seated.

"Nothing wrong with men in gauchos serving me food."

Benny grinned, "Is that sexist? I believe I may be offended."

She punched him on the shoulder. "If that's all it takes to offend you, I'm a lucky girl."

As soon as she said the words, she knew it was true. She was a lucky girl to have found a decent, dependable man. The fact that he was willing to step out of the box and experiment with food from different cultures was a bonus. Not that she minded eating alone, but it was so much more fun to hold out her fork and say "Oh, taste this."

Sharing. It wasn't something she was accustomed to, but it felt nice. Maybe for the first time she was willing to entertain the thought of one day sharing her life with another person.

Maybe.

Laura hated to spoil the mood, but she had to break the news to Benny. "Gabe is back at the shelter."

Benny jerked forward, at full attention. "Is he hurt again?"

"No." She held her hand up to keep Benny from freaking out. "It didn't work out with the foster family."

"Why not? He's a great kid. Any family would be lucky to have him. I wish…" he stopped there, but Laura knew what he was going to say.

"I know," she said. "Me too."

Benny glanced at his watch. "What do you say we skip dessert and go over for a visit?"

Laura's heart swelled. "I think that's a great idea."

After paying the check, Laura and Benny left the restaurant. Ten minutes later they were at Hyatt House. Gabe caught sight of them the moment they walked in the door, as if he'd been waiting at the window for them to arrive. He ran across the room and threw himself into Benny's arms, implicitly trusting that Benny would catch him.

Laura wished she could be that sure. But Gabe was still young. He hadn't had time for his heart to harden. He wasn't old enough to be cynical. For young Gabe, the world still held hope. He believed it would all turn out right and people wouldn't disappoint him over and over again.

There was a moment of doubt. Was she speaking for Gabe or herself? Maybe things could work out for Gabe somehow. Maybe it was her own experience growing up in the system that colored her thoughts.

She glanced at Gabe in Benny's arms, his little face pressed against the side of his neck. "I missed you," he said. "Forever and a half." He placed a hand on either side of Benny's face and looked directly into his eyes. "That place was stinky."

Benny knew he wasn't being literal but didn't press the point. It was probably selfish of him, but he'd missed the kid, too.

He set Gabe on the floor. "How's that arm," he asked.

"Good as new," Gabe said. But Benny could see he was favoring it. Time would heal the physical wound, but how long would Gabe carry the emotional scars?

Anger rose in Benny's chest. He wanted to protect Gabe and make sure nothing bad ever happened to him again.

"Hey Benny," Gabe said. "Did you know Miss Laura has a kitty? Her name is Dizzy."

"Daisy," Laura corrected, taking Gabe's other hand. Joined together, the three of them made their way into the community room.

"Yeah, Daisy. Like the flower. And, know what?"

"What?"

"I played with her and she rubbed her nose on my nose, like an Eskimo. Did you know that's how Eskimos kiss? I saw it in a book."

Benny smiled at Laura. "What kind of books do you have in the children's section?"

Gabe stared off into the distance. "Someday I'll have a cat and a dog and a rabbit."

Laura tilted her head. "Oh? What will you name them?"

Gabe had to think about that for a minute. "I'll name them all Buddy. Then when I say, 'Come here Buddy' they'll all come running and give me Eskimo kisses."

"That would save time," Benny agreed.

Just then, Carol came into the room. "Oh, you're here. I was hoping to ask you guys a favor."

Laura and Benny nodded in unison,

"I promised the kids a movie night and asked if they wanted popcorn with the movie." She shook her head. "They asked for donuts."

"I'm guessing you want us to make a donut run?"

Carol nodded. "If you wouldn't mind."

"Can I go too?" Gabe asked. "Can I? Please?"

Carol glanced from Gabe to Benny, then Laura. She lifted one shoulder and grinned. "Sure, I don't see why not." She blew a strand of hair from her face. "Honestly, I could use a bit of a sugar fix myself. Grab me a raspberry jelly donut, okay?"

"You got it," Benny said, then tipped his head. "Are you sure it's okay for us to take Gabe?

Carol shrugged. "You two are here so often you're practically employees. Put in a few more hours," she said jokingly, "and I can hire you as social workers, so yeah, it's okay."

When they left, Gabe skipped between them singing, "Donuts, donuts, razzle-berry donuts."

"That's a nice song," Laura said.

"I made it up."

Benny glanced at Laura and they shared a secret smile.

At the donut shop, Benny ordered three dozen assorted donuts, making sure there were a few "razzle-berries" included.

"What's your favorite?" he asked Laura.

"I can't choose a favorite," she admitted. "Then the others would feel left out."

Benny smiled. That was such a Laura thing to say.

"What about you?" she asked.

"Would it surprise you to hear I like a simple, plain donut?"

"Not surprised at all, Mr. Meat and Potatoes."

"That was the old me," he said. "My eyes have been opened by new dining experiences and now I'm ready to branch out where donuts are concerned." He pointed to the donut display. "What would you suggest?"

She thought about it for a moment. "How about a Bavarian Cream?"

Benny wasn't surprised. Of course, she'd choose something that sounded like it came from an exotic locale. "Two Bavarian Cream donuts," he told the server, then turned to Laura. "We'll travel together, okay?"

Gabe tugged on Benny's shirt. He leaned down and Gabe whispered in his ear. "Can we get one for Daisy?"

"No, pal. I'm afraid cats can't eat donuts, but I'll tell you what. Tomorrow I'll come by and we'll go to the pet store. You can pick out some cat treats and a toy or two for Daisy, okay?"

"Can we do it now?"

"Nope, the pet store is closed. But I promise we'll do it Monday, okay?"

"Promise?" Gabe's voice trembled.

Benny knew there were a lot of people who'd broken promises to the boy and vowed he'd never be one of them. "I promise," he said, holding Gabe's gaze. "You can count on me."

Gabe nodded, but Laura gave Benny a look that stopped him in his tracks. It seemed to be equal parts warning and apprehension.

He realized it wasn't just Gabe's trust he'd have to earn. He had to gain the trust of the little girl that still lived inside Laura who'd stopped expecting people to keep their promises.

****

The following Monday, Benny ran out on his lunch hour and picked up Gabe with Carol's blessing. At least he'd earned one person's trust.

At the pet store, Gabe couldn't decide between a

catnip mouse or a feathered bird on a string. "We can get both," Benny said.

Gabe's eyes widened. "We can? Both of them?"

Why not? It didn't take much to make Gabe happy and his smile went straight to Benny's heart. What would it hurt to spoil the boy a little? He paid for both toys as well as some kitten treats Gabe picked out.

Gabe stopped and stared at some brightly colored fish. Each one had its own little bowl to swim in and was marked with feathered fins and brilliant colors.

"Look how pretty," Gabe said, pressing his finger gently against the bowl. He turned his face up to Benny. "Do you think I could get one?"

"I don't know," Benny said in all honesty. "That's something we'd have to run by Ms. Carol. They may not be allowed to have pets there."

Gabe nodded his agreement. If it was up to Benny, he'd buy every fish in the store to make Gabe happy, but this wasn't his decision to make. He'd learned his lesson about making promises before checking with the people in authority.

With that issue put aside, Benny took Gabe's hand. "Let's go pay for these things and bring them to Laura and Daisy, okay?"

The bookstore was within walking distance from the pet shop. Gabe held Benny's hand and chattered the entire away. "Why are fire hydrants red?" He asked.

"I'm not sure," Benny said. "We can look it up to find out."

"You can Google it," Gabe said.

Benny chuckled. "Where'd you hear that?"

"My foster mother did a lot of Google."

"Yeah?" Benny's curiosity got the better of him.

"Was she nice to you?"

"She was at first." Gabe frowned. "Then she had her own real baby and was all don't touch the baby and don't get close to the baby and don't put your dirty hands near the baby and stuff." He took a deep breath and let it out with a sigh. "She really liked that baby a lot."

Benny wasn't sure how to respond, so he gently squeezed Gabe's hand a little tighter. When they reached the bookstore, Laura met them at the door.

Gabe held up the bag from the pet store. "We brought stuff for Daisy."

As if hearing her name, the kitten sprang across the room, half running and half hopping. Gabe went down on one knee and the kitten leaped into his arms. "There's a good girl," Gabe said, rubbing his cheek across the kitten's fur. They stayed that way in mutual adoration for a few minutes before Gabe reached into the bag and pulled out the feathered bird on a stick. He lifted it high and waved the bird back and forth. Daisy jumped and batted at the bird, causing Gabe to laugh aloud. "Look Benny. She likes it!"

Laura pulled Benny aside. "Carol must really trust you to take Gabe out."

"Well, we've gotten to know each other over the last few weeks."

Laura raised an eyebrow.

"No," Benny said, waving a hand in dismissal. "Not like that. I mean I've been spending time with Gabe and the other kids. I guess she knows my intentions are above board. I think she may be bending the rules a little for Gabe's sake."

"And yours." Laura nodded and changed the

subject. "She has good instincts. So does Nick, and he told me you were a good guy."

"He did? When was that?"

"Last Christmas. When he gave you the magic box."

Benny grunted.

"You still don't believe in magic?"

Benny tipped his head. "I believe in making my own magic, which is exactly what I'm doing."

He checked his watch. As much as he hated to break up Gabe's playtime with the kitten, it was time to return to work. "Ready to head back, Gabe?"

The boy looked up and pushed out his lower lip. "Already? We just got here." He snuggled the cat. "If I leave, Daisy won't have anyone to play with."

Laura bit her lips to keep from laughing. Gabe looked so serious. Even Daisy seemed to be waiting for an answer. She turned to Benny. Why don't you go on back to work and I'll let Carol know I'll bring Gabe back in a few hours?"

"Is that okay with you Gabe?"

Gabe nodded his head vehemently. "Yes, please."

"Okay," Benny said. "But you mind Miss Laura. And when she says it's time to go, no arguing. Deal?"

"Deal," Gabe said with a quick nod.

Benny simply stood there for a few minutes, as if he didn't want to leave. Finally, he turned to Laura. "Are we on for dinner this week?"

She shook her head. "No." Then, at his crestfallen expression, she added. "We're going to have lunch instead. And it's my surprise so I'll pick you up tomorrow at twelve o'clock."

"Tomorrow?"

"Yes, did you have other plans?"

"No, but…"

"I know. It's the fourth of July. I'll be packing a picnic lunch."

Benny looked into the distance. Laura knew he was thinking of those family picnics he missed so much. She was determined to make new memories for him so he wouldn't feel so alone.

His face brightened. "Okay," he said. "Sounds like fun,"

After saying goodbye to both Gabe and Daisy, Benny left to return to work. Laura watched Gabe playing with the kitten. This would work out perfectly. She wanted to talk to Carol anyway, and there were a few more things to put in place before Benny's surprise tomorrow.

Chapter Fourteen

Laura picked Benny up at precisely noon. He spotted a picnic basket in the back seat and imagined a romantic picnic with the two of them. While he was excited at the prospect of a day alone with Laura, this was a day that held so many memories for him. He missed his family and those crazy, hectic, fun-filled Fourth of July celebrations. He pushed the thought aside, determined to make the best of the day. Laura had gone to a lot of trouble and he wouldn't spoil it for her, no matter how much he missed his family.

They pulled up to a local park on the banks of Silver Lake Park. He couldn't have picked a more perfect spot for a picnic.

"They're having fireworks here tonight," she said, handing Benny the picnic basket. She took a rolled blanket and led the way. They rounded the corner and came to a covered pavilion. Benny stopped short. "What...?"

"Surprise!"

Benny looked from one familiar face to another—Sally and her friend Judy, Ivy from the bookstore, Carol from the shelter, and best of all, his little buddy Gabe.

He turned to Laura. "This is...I don't know how to thank you." He leaned forward, ready to show her how much he appreciated the trouble she went to, but before he could show her exactly how he felt, Gabe ran forward and threw himself into Benny's arms.

"Are you surprised Benny Penny?"

"Yes, so surprised."

"We're having a picnic, with hot dogs and hamburgers and potato salad and cornonacob and watermelon and fireworks and everything!"

"Wow." Benny turned to Laura. "Hot dogs and potato salad? What happened to eating around the world?"

Laura grinned. "America is part of the world."

Seeing the mountains of food spread across the picnic table, Benny lifted the picnic basket. "So, what's in here?"

Laura lifted one side of the basket. "Apple pie, of course."

"Of course."

"I like pie," Gabe said, pulling Benny toward the pavilion. "Wanna play Frisbee with me?"

Frisbee was followed by horseshoes, which was followed by eating and drinking, sparklers and laughter. Sitting on blankets and picnic tables with full tummies afterward, everyone settled down to watch the fireworks. The sky was ablaze with bursts of color accompanied by ooohs and aaahs.

Benny put his arm around Laura and pulled her close. It felt natural having her by his side while the fireworks brightened the sparkle in her eyes. "Thank you for a wonderful day," he said.

"You're welcome. I knew you'd be missing your family today."

He nodded. "Not as much now."

She leaned close and whispered in his ear. "Family

is not only about blood, but about who you invite into your heart." Her voice softened. "That's something you learn when you grow up without a family."

She was right, of course. This was the next best thing to a family picnic. He still missed his family, but he was surrounded by a new kind of family, people he'd welcomed into his life and people who'd chosen him to be a part of theirs as well. It wasn't all about blood, but about the people who loved and supported him.

He brushed his cheek against hers, inhaling the scent of her, a scent that was both exotic and familiar at the same time. He wanted more, but before he could capture her lips in a kiss, Gabe interrupted.

"Did you see that one?" he cried, pointing upward. "These are the best fireworks ever!" He looked from Benny to Laura and back, then blurted out. "I don't wanna go back. Can I go home with you? Please?"

Those pleading eyes nearly broke Benny's heart. He couldn't tell Gabe, but that was what he wanted as well. Lately he'd been envisioning himself as a husband and father. Holding Laura close, with Gabe on his lap, his vision took shape and form. A family. That was his final wish. If the box truly was magic, he'd fervently wish for a family this Christmas Eve.

It was nearly ten o'clock by the time the fireworks ended, and they'd packed up all the picnic supplies. Benny carried a sleepy Gabe to Carol's car. His eyes kept drifting closed, then they'd pop open and he'd ask if it was time to leave already.

"It's way past your bedtime, buddy."

A long sigh, then Gabe shut his eyes again and curled his face against Benny's shoulder. Benny strapped Gabe in, then thanked Carol for letting him share the day with them. She glanced at Laura, then back to Benny. "The three of you make a great team."

Benny couldn't agree more. He had a feeling it wouldn't take much to convince Laura of the same thing. They'd been getting closer these past few weeks and he was sure she was feeling the same things he was feeling. If things progressed the way Benny hoped they would, he wouldn't need a magic box to make his wish come true.

Benny and Laura hung back once everyone left. They sat on the blanket looking up at the stars. Benny placed his arm around her shoulder, and she leaned in to rest her head against his chest. "Thank you for a wonderful day," he said. "It means so much to me."

"I enjoyed it as much as you did. Besides, I wanted to take your mind off of missing your family."

"It did," he said. "But I have to tell you, as much as I miss my family, I've felt on the outside the last few years. Everyone is married, raising a family, and getting ahead in their careers. I felt I couldn't compete in a family of overachievers." He blew out a breath. "When the company went under, I could almost hear them saying, *Poor Benny, can't even hold onto a job.*"

She tilted her head up and gazed into his eyes. "You're not a failure to all those people who were here today. Each one of them admires you. And Gabe worships the ground you walk on."

Benny leaned close, barely brushing her lips with his own. "And you?"

"You're growing on me," she said with a soft chuckle, then wrapped her arms around his neck and kissed him fully and completely, giving him all the answer he needed. She leaned in for another kiss when the phone vibrated in her pocket. She tried to ignore it but couldn't concentrate on kissing Benny when her phone kept vibrating.

"One second," she said, pulling the phone from her pocket. When she saw the number of Sun Valley Assisted Living, she picked it up immediately. "This is Laura Bell," she said.

"Laura, this is Kim at Sun Valley. I'm afraid I have some bad news." She continued before Laura could interrupt. "It's Edna. She fell in the shower. She was unconscious when we found her."

"Oh my God." Laura jumped to her feet, nearly shouting into the phone. "Where is she?"

"She's at the hospital, Room 246."

"I'll be right there." Laura hung up the phone and grabbed her purse. Having heard her side of the conversation, Benny had already packed up the rest of their picnic supplies.

When they reached the car, he tossed everything in the back seat and held out his hand for the keys. "Let me drive," he said. "You're too upset."

Normally she would have argued, but her vision was blurred with tears. If anything happened to Edna. She couldn't even think of it.

"Edna is the closest thing I have to family," she said, her voice trembling. "She was going to adopt me, but before she could finalize the papers, she got sick. Everything fell apart. But papers or no papers, she always watched over me. Even after she got sick and had to sell Hyatt House."

Laura knew she was babbling but couldn't stop. She'd kept so many things inside for so long and now to have someone willing to listen, someone who really heard her, made all the difference in the world.

"There was never a more devoted, loving and kind woman in the universe." Laura's voice broke. "She would have been a fantastic mother."

They made it to the hospital in record time and Laura rushed to Edna's room, shocked to see how pale she was in the hospital bed. Her eyes were closed, and bandages covered most of her forehead. Tubes ran from her arm to a clear plastic bottle overhead.

Laura squeezed Edna's free hand. "I'm here now," she said, hoping Edna's eyes would flicker open and everything would be all right. They didn't. Laura had to lean in close to be sure Edna was breathing. "Please," she begged. "Please be all right."

****

The sun's early rays had begun to turn the sky to gold when Edna stirred. Laura, who had been drifting in and out of sleep in a chair beside the bed, sat straight up. "Hey," she said.

Edna blinked her eyes and cleared her throat. "What happened?"

"You fell and hit your head."

Edna reached up to touch the bandages on her head, then winced. "Hurts."

Laura poured her a glass of water. "They said you don't have a concussion."

"Feels like I don't have a head." She squinted her eyes in Benny's direction. "Who's this?"

"Just a friend."

Benny stood. "Laura's told me so much about you."

Edna narrowed her eyes, "She forgot to mention

you."

"This is Benjamin. We're just friends," Laura repeated.

"Help me up," Edna said. Before Laura could stand, Benny was at her side. He slipped one arm beneath Edna and helped her sit up straighter. He tucked the pillow at the base of her spine and adjusted it until she was comfortable.

"You know, you could have hit this button to raise the bed," Laura said.

They both ignored her. "So, Benjamin, what is it you do?"

"I work at Sun Valley Country Club."

"Oh, do you like it there?"

"Love it," Benny admitted.

"And the job pays well?"

Laura gasped. "Edna!"

"It's okay," Benny said. "I started at the bottom and worked my way up. I've gotten a few promotions along the way and I'm making a very comfortable living now. As a matter of fact," he cast a glance at Laura. "I've been able to put away enough for a down payment on a house. A really nice house with a yard. Big enough for a family one day."

"Really?" Edna studied him more closely. "Family man, huh?"

Benny thought about it for a minute, then nodded. "Yeah, I guess I am."

"Good. Now I'm getting tired again. Why don't you two run along and let this old lady get some rest." With that she lay back and closed her eyes, but Benny saw her lips curl up in a smile and knew he had her seal of approval.

****

Over the next few months, Benny and Laura made regular visits to Edna's bedside. Sometimes Benny would read to Edna and other times Laura would read.

By the time fall came around, it was evident Edna's health was failing, and it broke his heart to see the effect it was having on Laura. He'd grown attached to Edna as well and could understand why Laura was so devoted. Maybe if things had been different and Edna hadn't gotten sick all those years ago, Laura wouldn't be so cautious about letting anyone into her heart. Each time he felt she'd let her guard down a bit, another wall stood rock solid right behind it.

Benny was determined to be the one Laura let inside. Their Sunday-morning breakfasts had become a regular event now, as well as dinners at restaurants he would never have tried without her guidance. More and more it seemed as if she was opening up and willing to trust him.

Trust.

He'd put his trust in the box as Nick had suggested, and he'd found the woman of his dreams. He remembered telling Nick the day they'd met that security to him meant a roof over his head, a regular income, a fulfilling job, food on the table, and good friends he could count on.

Benny had all those things. The only thing missing was someone to share it with. The thought of proposing to Laura sent him into a spin. There was nothing he wanted more. But he'd felt that way once before. He'd been blindsided by Melody's lies, too smitten to see the truth. The sense of betrayal still burned, but he hadn't fallen for her manipulations a second time. Now she was out of his life for good.

But Laura wasn't Melody. She'd never hurt him the way he'd been hurt in the past. Benny was ready to make that leap again. He bought a small diamond ring. Nothing as fancy as the one Edna had given to Laura, but it was the one she'd ultimately wear on the third finger of her left hand. And this time the ring he put on a woman's finger would represent love, fidelity and, above all, honesty.

There was only one thing left to do and that would be taken care of this morning. When he arrived at the doorstep of his soon-to-be new home, Opal Grainger and her husband Hal greeted him. He walked inside and felt the same way he'd felt the first time he'd entered the quaint farmhouse. It had felt like home then and it felt like home now.

He imagined Sunday breakfasts on the long oak table, a row of Christmas stockings hung over the fireplace, and wall-to-wall shelves for Laura's prized book collection. It was perfect.

Opal gave Benny a warm hug and Hal shook his hand. They'd become friends over the past few months. Benny had contacted his parents and together they'd helped the Grainger's find the perfect retirement home in Florida. Their dream was coming true.

And so was his. With his excellent credit rating and the down payment he'd been able to save, he'd secured a mortgage for the house they'd lovingly sold. Unfortunately, it had taken every penny he'd saved, and he wouldn't be able to buy airline tickets to visit his family over the holidays as he'd hoped. But that was a small price to pay for the privilege of owning his own home.

175

They'd signed the papers the week before, and the Grainger's asked if they could stay a few days until the moving van came. Benny had no problem with that and told them they were welcome to stay as long as they needed.

Opal had tears in her eyes. "I'm glad you bought the house," she said. "I know you'll love it as much as we did."

"I will," Benny replied.

Hal slapped Benny on the back. "I hope you'll be as happy here as we have. This place is full of wonderful memories."

Benny nodded. "I intend to make more wonderful memories here. And you know you're welcome to come back and stay here anytime you're visiting the area. There are plenty of bedrooms."

For now, anyway.

He hoped Laura wanted a big family as well. If so, they'd soon fill the house with the sound of children's laughter, and Benny's life would be complete.

He helped the Grainger's move the last of their personal items to their car. They planned to drive to their new home and visit several vacation spots along the way. Handing over the keys, they left with a hug and a wave and Benny was alone to walk through his new home.

It was quiet, the kind of quiet that comes with peace and calm. Outside the wind rustled the leaves of a massive oak tree and fallen leaves skittered underfoot. The large back yard was fenced in. Benny imagined a set of swings, and in his imagination, it was Gabe flying forward and back, kicking his legs out and laughing. Maybe they'd have a dog as well.

The Grainger's left a lot of their furniture behind, claiming they had to downsize. He planned on leaving most of the decorating up to Laura. He wouldn't be moving in right away, anyway.

He'd been a little concerned about leaving Sally behind, but he'd thought of the perfect solution. Once he and Laura were married, Laura would move into the house and Sally could have the apartment over the bookstore. That way she wouldn't be alone during the day and he could check in on her in the evening when he picked Laura up from work. It was a perfect solution.

He couldn't wait for Laura to see. But for now, it would be his secret. He planned to propose on Christmas Eve, then he'd surprise her with the perfect house, the house just waiting for them to move into.

It would be his Christmas present to his future fiancée.

Chapter Fifteen

Laura was numb. Empty. Edna was gone and there were arrangements to be made. But not tonight. Operating on autopilot, she left the hospital, stopping only when a nurse asked her to sign out Edna's belongings.

"And this," the nurse said. "She wanted you to have this."

The letter with her name scrawled across the front was almost too much. Laura tucked it into the bag holding Edna's belongings, which was surprisingly light. But then, Edna's needs had been few these last few weeks.

There was only one person Laura wanted to be with, one person who would understand the depth of her pain and loss. She rushed to Benny's apartment, falling into his arms when he opened the door. And then, finally the tears came in a torrent of heartbreak. She cried until she couldn't cry any more while Benny held her close, murmuring soft words of comfort.

When the tears finally stopped, Benny walked her to the couch and handed her a box of tissues. "I'm sorry," she said, blowing her nose. "I must look a mess."

He rubbed her back. "You look like someone who's lost a person they loved."

Laura shook her head slowly from side to side. "I thought nothing could ever hurt me again. I'd gotten so used to being abandoned, that I'd closed off my feelings. Or I thought I had."

"You loved her. And she loved you in return."

Laura gave a slow nod. "That's why I'd taught myself not to love. If you don't love someone it can't hurt you when they leave."

"Oh honey. Edna didn't leave because she wanted to."

"I know, but the pain is the same. She's gone." Laura gave an angry swipe to her tear-stained cheeks. "One more person ripped out of my life. One more empty space that can never be filled. One more night of wondering why I'm always left behind. Why I don't deserve to be loved?"

Benny took her chin in his hand and lifted her face to his. "You *do* deserve to be loved. I love you, Laura."

She wanted to believe him, but those old tapes kept playing through her head. *You're unwanted, unlovable. You don't deserve to be happy.*

She turned her face away, avoiding Benny's gaze. This wasn't the time to deal with his proclamation. She was too raw inside. Too vulnerable. "I have to go," she said. "I'm sorry."

"Laura, stay. Please."

She stood and turned to leave. "We'll talk later. I promise. I have too much on my mind right now."

****

Once home, she made a list of all the things that needed to be done—from making funeral arrangements to cleaning out Edna's rooms at the assisted living home. She tried to preoccupy herself with details in order to push thoughts of Benny out of her mind. Nick had been right. Benny was one of the good guys. And maybe right now he believed that he did love her but believing it herself was treading on dangerous ground. It would only set her up for heartache in the future, because everyone she loved left her eventually. That was the truth she'd learned from the day she'd been abandoned at Hyatt House.

Laura carried Edna's bag of belongings to the countertop. She couldn't deal with it at the moment. An envelope with her name on it caught her attention. She pulled it out and opened the envelope, her heart breaking when she saw Edna's familiar spidery scrawl.

My darling Laura,

If you're reading this, I've moved on. I'm not afraid. This is the next step in my journey and I'm looking forward to whatever comes next. My only regret is that this disease kept me from adopting you as I'd planned. Even without the paperwork you were, and will always be, the daughter of my heart.

Remember that, dear Laura. You were loved and you deserve to be loved. Don't let your past get in the way of your future. Promise me you'll let love in. That Benjamin seems like a nice young man.

Laura wiped a tear from her eye. Edna's words hit close to home. Not enough to tear down her walls, but more subtle, like silken veils drifting to the floor, one at a time, leaving her feeling exposed and vulnerable.

She turned to the second page, where Edna explained that she'd named Laura sole beneficiary of her insurance policy, a policy she'd bought as a young bride decades ago. Over the years the value had increased to... Laura gulped. She dropped into a nearby chair, stunned beyond words.

Nearly a quarter of a million dollars! That would pay off the mortgage on the bookstore and all of her bills. She would never have to worry again.

I hope that this money will solve your financial issues and ease some of your fears. I know it won't make up for growing up the way you did, but at least you'll never have to depend on anyone else for your happiness.

Laura wiped tears from her eyes. Yes, the money would solve her financial issues. But she'd give it all up to have Edna back.

Chapter Sixteen

Autumn came, and with it a chill settled in the air. By November the trees had lost most of their leaves and the skies had turned gray. Laura still missed Edna but was grateful for the money she'd provided. With her bills paid, the store ownership in her name, and a healthy bank account for a cushion, most of Laura's worries were behind her. Edna had left her the gift of security and that was something Laura had spent her life searching for.

That wasn't all Edna had left, however. She'd left the kind of advice a mother would give about learning to trust. Laura reread Edna's letter nearly every single day. Lately she'd felt more and more ready to take that leap of faith.

Her thoughts turned to Benny. He was honest, trustworthy and kind. He'd make a wonderful husband and father one day. The mere fact that Laura was willing to entertain the idea proved how far she'd come. Benny had been her rock during Edna's funeral and afterward when she'd struggled with having lost the closest person to a family member she had.

That loss made her even more aware of how Benny must feel being separated from his family. He'd talked about going to Florida for a family reunion over Thanksgiving, but something had come up. Benny didn't elaborate. He simply said the money was better used elsewhere. But she had money now and had purchased an open-ended, round-trip ticket for him to make the trip over the Christmas holidays.

She knew that Edna would approve.

Laura smiled in anticipation as she helped Benny prepare a Thanksgiving feast. They'd decided there would be more room at his apartment, and it would be more convenient for Sally, so she'd brought all the groceries over early that morning and they'd started preparations. She and Benny worked well together, moving around the kitchen like a choreographed dance. Benny chopped vegetables, sautéed mushrooms and stirred up dishes Laura had never heard of.

It was the first time she'd made Thanksgiving dinner and she wanted it to be perfect. She'd been saving recipes to her Pinterest board for weeks. Sally was bringing pie and Carol was making a sweet potato casserole. Laura had made fresh yeast rolls and picked up a jar of turkey gravy just in case her gravy came out lumpy and tasteless.

But the bird. That was the centerpiece of the table. She'd slathered it in butter, stuffed it with sausage dressing and sent up a prayer to the divine cooking gods that it would come out moist and delicious.

It would be a small, intimate dinner—Benny, Sally and Lou, Nick and Beverley, and Carol, who couldn't guarantee she'd be able to bring Gabe along, but promised to try. Laura set the table for eight, hoping Gabe would be there.

When she came back into the kitchen, Benny was throwing ingredients into a bowl. "What are you making?" she asked.

"This is my mother's famous green bean casserole. It's a staple at our Thanksgiving dinner table." His smile held a hint of sadness. "It wouldn't be Thanksgiving without it."

"It's nice that you'll have a piece of your family tradition at the table today."

"And making new traditions," he said. He peeked inside the oven and took a deep breath. "Smells wonderful."

She crossed her fingers and smiled. "Let's hope it tastes wonderful too." She turned and suddenly his arms were around her waist. She tipped her face to his and their lips met in a long, lingering kiss.

When they pulled apart, Benny smiled. "Your cheeks are red. Is it hot in here, or is it me?"

Laura leaned in for another kiss. "A little of both." She slipped out of his embrace. "Wine?" Without waiting for an answer, she poured them each a glass. They toasted to the holidays and many more to come.

"This is one of my father's favorite toasts," Benny said, touching his glass to Laura's. "Here's to good old turkey, the bird that comes each fall, and with his sweet, persuasive meat, makes gobblers of us all."

Laura smiled. She couldn't imagine what it must have been like growing up in a family that had silly Thanksgiving toasts and traditional once-a-year casseroles. For some reason, the thought didn't carry the same feelings of regret it would have in the past. She loved hearing Benny talk about his family and thought maybe one day they'd make memories and traditions of their own.

She took a sip of wine, then set her glass on the counter. "I want to give you something before everyone else gets here."

"Another kiss?" he asked.

"Maybe later." She laughed at his playful pout. "This is an early Christmas gift. Now close your eyes."

Benny did as he was told. He heard Laura slip away, then return. "Hold out your hand."

He held out his hand and something light dropped into his palm. "Can I open my eyes now?"

"Yes."

He opened his eyes and looked at an envelope with his name on it. It was decorated with Christmas stickers. When he opened the envelope, his jaw dropped. "Airline tickets?"

"I know how much you wanted to be at your family's Christmas reunion. I think Edna would be thrilled to know some of her money was going to make that happen."

Benny was stunned at the gesture. Yes, he had talked about flying to Florida for the reunion, but it was more important to put a down payment on the house and get Laura a ring. He'd planned to propose at Christmas, but if he was going to fly home for Christmas, maybe he'd have to make the proposal an early Christmas present as well.

"Thank you," he said, pulling her into his arms. "This is the most thoughtful and generous thing anyone has ever done for me."

"I just want you to be happy."

"I am," he said, meaning every word he said. "You make me happy." He almost got down on his knees then and there, but he didn't have the ring yet. The final installment would be made the week before Christmas and he'd intended to propose on Christmas Eve. It seemed appropriate since that was the anniversary of the day they met. He had another ulterior motive as well. If Laura agreed to marry him, he'd make his final wish at midnight—a wish for a family of his own.

It was just as well he didn't have the ring to propose because the guests began to arrive and Benny was in charge of making sure everyone had drinks— wine, soft drinks, or a cranberry punch concoction Laura had made.

Nick arrived, along with his wife Beverley. "Lovely to meet you again," she said, then handed Benny a floral centerpiece in autumn colors—vibrant red, orange and gold.

Benny thanked them both, then leaned forward. "I kind of miss the Santa outfit."

A mischievous grin lit up Nick's face. "Only a month away," he said. "My favorite time of the year."

Beverley excused herself and joined Laura in the kitchen. Benny placed the flowers on the center of the table. It was exactly the finishing touch they needed. "Thank you," he said. "They're perfect."

"That's not all," Nick said, holding out a covered tray. "I brought deviled eggs."

"Of course. What else would an egg farmer bring? Do you have any other skills I don't know about?"

"I do a little woodworking."

"Oh? Do you make toys by any chance?"

Nick's blue eyes twinkled. "Actually, I do. I hold a woodworking class once a month. We make wooden puzzles, trains and toys that we donate to the local schools."

Benny grinned. "Your friends wouldn't be elves, would they?"

Nick lifted his gaze up and tapped his chin. "Hmmm...well Theodore is short, but I wouldn't call him an elf. Nope, just regular guys who like working with wood."

"Which one of you made the box?"

"You mean the magic box?"

"The jury is still out on that one."

"To tell the truth, none of us made it. That box has been handed down by my father and his father before him. The rules haven't changed. The box grants three wishes, then I pass it on to a new person as my father and his father before him did."

Benny furrowed his brow. "One thing I've been meaning to ask you. Why'd you pick me?"

Nick shrugged. "Sometimes you just know." He winked. "Call it Santa Sense."

Benny shook his head. "Funny thing. I didn't see my name on the box when you first gave it to me."

"That's part of the magic," Nick said. "The name only appears when the person receiving it agrees to use it. The fact that your name appeared means you chose, whether consciously or unconsciously, to make your wishes." He glanced at Laura. "It looks as if a few of your wishes have come true. So why would the jury still be out on whether or not the box is magic?"

"Well, it seems to me that I did everything I needed to get what I wanted. The box only provided the tools. I did all the work."

"Isn't that what magic is?"

"I guess if you look at it that way. All I know is that sometimes magic is simply knowing what you want." He glanced at Laura. "Or being in the right place at the right time. If I hadn't come to the community center for a hot meal last Christmas, none of this would have happened."

"Magic," Nick said, with a nod of his head.

Before they could continue the conversation, Sally showed up carrying the most perfect apple pie Benny had ever seen. The crust was golden brown with a basket weave top crust and perfectly crimped edges. She'd also brought along a date.

"This is my friend Lou," she said. "Lou, this is Benny, the young man I've been telling you about."

"Pleased to meet you," Lou said, reaching out to shake his hand.

Benny gave Lou the once-over but stopped short of asking what his intentions were. Lou seemed like a nice enough guy, and if Sally was ready to move on, she certainly didn't need his blessing.

Benny took the pie from Sally. "Wow, this is a work of art, Sally."

She blushed at the compliment. "I wasn't sure if everyone liked cheddar cheese on their pie or ice cream, so I bought both."

"I'm an ice cream guy," Benny said.

"Cheese." Nick called out.

Benny turned. "Nick, have you met my neighbor Sally…and her friend Lou?"

Nick tipped an imaginary cap, "I don't believe I've had the pleasure." He took the pie from Benny's hands and placed it on the table. "Can I get you a drink? I believe Laura said she was making her famous cranberry punch."

"That sounds delightful," Sally said and the three of them wandered over to the drink station. Soon they were joined by Sally's friends Ivy and Judy. Nick seemed perfectly comfortable entertaining the women. But then, who didn't love jolly old St. Nick? Benny thought with a smile.

He glanced up and caught Laura's gaze. They were probably thinking the same thing. Would Carol bring Gabe? He knew Laura would be disappointed if Gabe wasn't here to share their Thanksgiving. So would he.

More than any other holiday, Thanksgiving was all about family. Sharing food, fun and laughter. He didn't have his own family here, but as Laura had once said, family was about who you invited into your heart, not solely the family you were born into.

Then there were the airline tickets Laura had given him. The gesture touched him in ways he couldn't fully express. That thoughtful, caring heart was one of the things he loved about her and one of the reasons she'd make the perfect life partner.

The doorbell rang and Benny was at the door in moments. When he opened the door, Gabe jumped into his arms. "Happy Turkey Day!"

"Happy Turkey Day to you too, buddy."

"Do you know what the turkey says?"

"What?"

"Gobble, gobble, gobble."

Benny put Gabe down, and he quickly turned and ran off to tell Laura what a turkey says. Benny turned to Carol and mouthed a silent "thank you."

Together they went into the kitchen where Gabe was showing Laura the things he had in his backpack— a coloring book and crayons, two dinosaur books and his favorite rock.

"What makes that rock so special?" she asked.

He turned it over and held it out. "See this spot

here? It looks like a heart."

Laura looked at it carefully. "Why, I do believe you're right."

"I know. It's a love rock."

He tucked his treasures back inside his backpack, then asked Laura if he could help.

"Yes, please." She handed him a tray of cheese and crackers. "Could you bring this to the table? And Benny, could you help me lift this turkey out of the oven? I think it's an eighty-pounder."

Benny chuckled and reached for the potholders. "Thirteen to be exact. But who's counting."

Laura gave him a good-natured swat with the dish towel.

Benny lifted the turkey out of the oven. It was golden brown and cooked to perfection. He covered it with foil while Laura put casseroles in the oven. Just then Sally poked her head in. "Anything I can do?"

Laura gave her a hopeful glance. "How are you at making gravy?"

"Well, I don't like to brag, but…"

"You're hired," Laura said. "I've never made gravy."

"Let me show you my no-fail method."

Seeing how Sally had taken Laura under her wing, Benny went into the living room to see how the rest of their guests were making out. Carol and Ivy were discussing a reality show about housewives while Nick asked Gabe about school.

Gabe answered politely, all the while staring at Nick. Finally, unable to hold it in any longer, he blurted out, "Did you know you look kinda like Santa Claus?"

"Really? Doesn't Santa wear a red suit?"

"Yeah, but…"

"And doesn't he wear glasses?"

"I guess."

"So, I look a little like Santa, but not exactly."

"Uh huh."

Nick patted Gabe on the head. "Thank you for telling me."

"You're welcome," Gabe said, still not entirely convinced. Benny caught him staring at Nick with a suspicious look on his face, but he didn't bring the subject up again.

Benny distracted the boy with an appetizer. "Did you ever eat ants on a log?"

Gabe's eyes widened. "No."

"Here." Benny held out a celery stick with peanut butter and raisins. "My mother used to make these for a snack when I got home from school."

Gabe studied the celery. "They're not real ants."

"Nope. We only called it that because the raisins look like ants."

Gabe took a bite and nodded his approval. "It's good."

"Do you want to take the tray around and offer some to people?"

"Can I?"

"Sure."

Benny handed the tray to Gabe, then watched as he offered them to their guests. He heard Gabe assure everyone that they weren't made with real ants. Benny turned to Nick. "That was a close call. Gabe almost figured out you were Santa."

Nick nodded. "It wouldn't have mattered. He would have found a way to justify why Santa Claus was eating turkey with him at Thanksgiving. Kids are highly adaptable, especially when their belief system is in jeopardy." Nick placed a hand on Benny's shoulder. "They believe because they *want* to believe, not because someone told them they have to."

"So, we're back to me believing in magic, huh?"

"You're the one who keeps bringing it up."

Before Benny could argue the point, Laura called him to the kitchen. He made his escape and joined her in the kitchen. "I think everything is about ready now. Could you carve the turkey?"

"Absolutely." He pulled the carving knife out of the drawer, grateful that he'd thought to pick one up at the local department store. He couldn't remember the last time he'd had to carve anything.

"Taste this first," Sally said, holding out a spoonful of gravy. She blew on it first, then lifted the spoon to his mouth. "Does it need salt?" she asked.

Benny moaned when the gravy hit his taste buds. "Oh Sally. It's perfect. Just perfect."

"You're not just saying that, are you?"

"Nope. You should bottle this and sell it."

Sally beamed with pride when Benny sliced off a bit of turkey breast and dipped it into the gravy. "I could eat this on everything."

"Not my apple pie," she said with a smile.

"Okay, but everything else is going to be swimming in gravy." He caught Laura looking at him in the same way his mother used to when he brought home a good report card. A sense of homesickness washed over him. Then he remembered the airline tickets Laura had given him. He'd see his family soon, thanks to her.

He finished carving the turkey, grateful that he'd

looked up the carving technique on the internet the night before. When he finished, he carried the platter of turkey to the table where Sally and Laura were placing an assortment of covered casserole dishes. Soon everyone was seated and raising their glasses for a toast.

"To family and friends," Benny said.

"And those we've lost," Laura added.

Nick raised his glass "To Edna."

Benny had forgotten that Nick knew both Edna and Laura. He'd have to talk to Nick later and find out more about Laura as a child. But for now, conversation centered around Thanksgiving traditions.

Sally told them about one of her family's traditions. She passed out slips of paper and asked everyone to write down one thing for which they were thankful. They tossed all the slips of paper into a wooden bowl and passed the bowl around the table. Each person reached in and took out a slip of paper to read.

When he pulled out a slip, Benny read aloud. "I'm grateful for cookies and my friends and for Santa Claus and cranberry sauce." There was a drawing of a dinosaur, as if Benny couldn't figure out who wrote it. He felt a lump in his throat.

"Miss Laura helped me write it," Gabe said. "But I drew the dinosaur all by myself."

"You did a great job." Benny passed the slip of paper around the table and everyone agreed it was the best dinosaur drawing they'd ever seen. "Maybe you'll be an artist one day."

"I already am," Gabe stated. "I did three drawings today already."

And if that didn't make you an artist, Benny thought. What did?

After dinner Sally asked Carol to run across the hall with her to bring over the ice cream, cheese and whipped cream for her apple pie. Benny helped Laura clear the table and stack dishes.

"Carol brought another bottle of wine. Could you open it?"

Unfortunately, this one had a cork rather than a screw-off cap. And as far as Benny knew, he didn't own a corkscrew. "Hold on," he said. "Maybe Sally has one."

Benny walked across the hall but stopped at Sally's door when he heard his name mentioned.

"Yes, it's obvious they both adore the boy. I told Laura she should have one of those...what do they call it in the books? A 'marriage of convenience' right?"

"Oh," Sally exclaimed. "I love those stories! Yes, that's the perfect solution."

Benny backed up quietly, his heart pounding in his chest. Marriage of convenience? A perfect solution? Is that all he was to Laura? He stepped back inside his apartment, feeling the world telescope around him until there was nothing but memories of pain and betrayal. It was happening all over again.

Laura had lied to him. The pain was just as sharp and shocking as it was the first time when he'd found out Melody had been lying to him. Maybe more so because he'd tied all his hopes and dreams up into this relationship, confident that lightning wouldn't strike twice.

A marriage of convenience. Laura didn't care about him at all. He was just a means to an end. Benny felt like a fool and he had sworn never to let a woman make a fool of him again.

"Hey Benny." Gabe tugged on his shirt. "When do we get pie?"

"Um. Soon. Soon." He could see Ivy and Laura in the kitchen starting the dishes. That was the last place he wanted to be.

Nick ambled over and gave Benny a sharp glance. "Everything all right?"

"Hmmm…?"

"You're looking a little pale."

"Yeah." Benny rubbed his stomach. "Something's not sitting right, that's all."

Nick nodded, but it was obvious he didn't believe a word Benny said.

"Hey, could you do me a favor? Would you run across the hall and ask Sally if she has a corkscrew to open that wine in the kitchen? I'm going to take some antacid."

He wasn't really. He needed a few moments alone to digest what he'd heard. Alone in the bathroom, he took some deep breaths trying to wrap his mind around the conversation he'd overheard. Just how long had Carol and Laura been concocting this plan to trick him into a marriage of convenience? How long had Laura been playing with his emotions, pretending to be attracted to him when instead he was only a means to an end? His stomach clenched and acid burned the pit of his throat, but it wasn't something an antacid could fix. It was the pain of betrayal striking him all over again.

****

It was another hour or so before everyone went

home, leaving Benny and Laura alone in the apartment. They washed and dried the dishes in silence. Laura could tell something was wrong. She couldn't imagine what might have happened to cause Benny's mood to shift so suddenly.

He wiped the countertop and hung the dish rag over the sink. "I guess that's it. Thanks for your help."

Laura knew the signs of rejection. She'd lived with them all of her life. It was evident Benny didn't want her there. "I guess I'll be going," she said, hoping he'd stop her.

He didn't. "Here," he said, holding out the tickets she'd given him. "Take these with you."

She stared into his eyes, but they were blank, dismissing her as if she meant nothing to him. "Benny, I don't understand."

He shook his head. "I was ready to give you the world. I thought I could trust you. But you lied to me, and you can't build a future based on lies."

"What do you mean?"

"I overheard Carol telling Sally about your plans to marry me so you could adopt Gabe. I never meant anything to you, did I?"

"Plans? I don't understand."

"Don't pretend you don't know what I'm talking about. You've been lying to me all along. Just like…" He didn't finish the sentence, but Laura knew what he was talking about. He thought she was no better than the woman who'd cheated on him.

Her emotions went from hurt to angry. "You think I'm a liar and a cheat? I thought you knew me better than that."

"I thought so too. I guess I was wrong." He turned

his back on her, shutting her out.

She turned on her heel. "If that's the way you feel, go ahead. Turn your back on me, just like everyone else. I should have known you were no different than the rest."

With that she stormed, not giving either of them a chance to explain. What was left to say?

Chapter Seventeen

The next few weeks were miserable. Instead of looking forward to Christmas, Benny dreaded it. The ring he'd bought for Laura sat on his dresser, mocking him. In hindsight, maybe he'd overreacted, but the pain of betrayal had reared up and caused him to say things he now regretted.

Maybe he could have handled things differently. Now that he'd had some time to think about it, he regretted his knee-jerk reaction. He'd assumed the worst based on past experience without giving Laura a chance to explain. He couldn't take all the blame, however. Instead of defending herself, Laura had fallen back into her own familiar patterns and shut him out. She'd assumed he was no better than everyone else who'd let her down in the past.

Maybe there was still hope they could resolve their differences. Maybe if he could talk to her. But his stubborn pride kept him from taking the first step. He was the one who'd been lied to. *She* should apologize to him.

That Christmas Eve, Benny not only donated several turkeys to the community center, but also an enormous box of gifts for Santa to give to the children. He almost didn't show up but couldn't help himself. His visit was dampened by the fact that Laura wouldn't look him in the eye and Gabe was acting suspiciously.

"Hey buddy, what's up?"

"Nothin," Gabe said, avoiding eye contact. Was Gabe upset that he and Laura had broken up?

Benny was about to leave when Nick stopped him. "Leaving already?"

"Yeah, it doesn't feel as if I'm welcome here."

"Don't assume," Nick chastised. "Things are not always what they seem."

Benny glanced across the room, but Laura had her back to them. "Sometimes things are exactly what they seem," he countered.

Nick grasped his arm. "Remember what I told you? Trust the box, Benny."

"Yeah, the box. Whatever."

Even as he rejected the idea, a part of him was sorely tempted. Nick's constant assertions that the box held magical properties were finally getting to him. Or maybe he was desperate. What harm would come from wishing things could go back to the way they were before the Thanksgiving fiasco?

As midnight drew closer, the temptation to make a Christmas Eve wish grew stronger. Finally giving in to the urge, Benny went in search of the box. It wasn't where he left it. He searched high and low, but the box couldn't be found.

He emptied dresser drawers, checked all around his desk and even searched the kitchen cabinets. And now that he couldn't find it that was all he could think about. It was as if he'd lost his last chance at happiness.

He recalled seeing it at Thanksgiving, but not since. Could someone have moved it? Worse yet, had someone stolen it?

As midnight came and went, Benny realized it didn't matter. Even a magic box wouldn't be able to grant him the one wish he had been planning to make this year. He stayed awake for hours, unable to sleep. He tossed and turned, haunted by dreams of being alone forever.

****

Christmas morning held no charm for Laura. Even the fashion doll sitting on her shelf seemed despondent in her Christmas finery. Why hadn't she just told Benny the truth? She'd never agreed to a marriage of convenience. That was all Carol's idea. But instead of explaining, she'd let those old fears of abandonment take over and cause her to act out like a child having a tantrum. She couldn't even visit Edna to cheer herself up. She missed her even more today.

But she couldn't stand the thought of sitting in her apartment all alone on Christmas day. So, she got dressed, pasted a smile on her face and went over to the shelter with a basket of books for the children. There was nothing like a child's laughter to chase the blues away.

When she arrived at the shelter, most of the children were in the game room. A lopsided artificial Christmas tree stood in the corner. There were pieces of torn wrapping paper under the tree and toys scattered around—building blocks, games, dolls and plastic robots. She knew the community usually donated gifts to the shelter, but this seemed like more than usual.

"Anonymous donation," Carol said, as if reading her mind.

"Anonymous, huh?" She suspected who this anonymous donor might be, and figured Carol had her own suspicions as well.

"So, how is Benny?" she asked, confirming Laura's suspicions.

She shrugged. "Haven't seen much of him since Thanksgiving." She hadn't told Carol what he'd overheard and had no intention of mentioning it. No sense having her feel bad as well. "We're both busy with Christmas and all."

Carol gave her a questioning look, but Laura changed the subject. She placed the basket of books under the tree with the other gifts and told the children to choose one to keep. She looked around the room, but there was no sign of Gabe. "Has anyone seen Gabe?" she asked.

One of the girls raised her hand. "He went back to his room. I think he was crying."

Oh, no. Laura's chest tightened. She knew holidays were the hardest in here, even surrounded by people acting happy and cheerful. Carol turned but Laura stopped her. "Let me," she said. "I know how he's feeling." She rushed to Gabe's room and found him sitting on his bed, tears streaming down his face.

She sat beside him and put an arm around his shoulder, feeling his body shake with suppressed sobs. "What's wrong, sweetie?"

"It didn't work." His voice hitched. "Stupid, stupid box."

She held him close. "It's okay, Gabe. Everything's going to be okay." Then she saw the box on his lap, the one with Benny's name on the front. How had it gotten here?

Gabe put his hand over the box, but it was too late.

"Where did you get this?"

Gabe looked away. "I just wanted to make a wish at midnight like Santa said. But it didn't work. The stupid box isn't magic. I wished for a family and nothing happened."

Laura understood the idea of wanting something with that much intensity, something that seemed so far out of reach. She wanted something that way, as well. She wanted Benny, and she was going to tell him that, even if it meant risking rejection again.

"Oh Gabe. This doesn't belong to you. You know we have to take the box back to Benny, right?"

Gabe squeezed his eyes shut and shook his head. "He's gonna be mad at me."

"We'll explain. He won't be mad. I promise." She knew Benny would forgive Gabe. But would he listen to her, too? Yes, she knew in her heart that it was true. Benny would understand if they just explained. He wasn't a heartless or vindictive person. Why hadn't she realized that weeks ago.

"Get your coat," she told Gabe. "We're going to visit Benny and bring the box back to him."

****

Benny jumped when the doorbell rang. Too late, he realized there wouldn't be a present on his doorstep this year. Not without the magic wishing box. He opened the door, surprised to see Laura and Gabe.

Laura held out a fruitcake. "This was on your doorstep," she said. Then she turned to Gabe. "Do you have something to tell Benny?"

Gabe nodded with a serious expression on his face.

"Come inside," Benny said. "It's cold out here."

They followed Benny inside and sat on the living room couch. Gabe opened his backpack and pulled out

Benny's missing box. Benny's gaze traveled from Gabe holding the magic box to Laura holding the fruitcake. He'd forgotten Nick's most important command: *Trust the box.*

Gabe shoved the box into Benny's hands. "Take it," he said. "Stupid thing doesn't work."

"Where did you get this?"

"I found it on Thanksgiving and put it in my backpack to make a wish."

"Stealing is wrong, Gabe."

"I didn't steal it," Gabe said, looking down and shuffling his feet. "I just borrowed it to make a wish, and I was gonna bring it back." He looked up at Benny and his lower lip trembled. "Santa said it was magic. I stayed up until both hands on the clock were pointing straight up. Miss Carol said that's when it was midnight. Then I made my wish. I wished for a family..." His voice trailed off to a whisper. "I wished for *us* to be a family." His lips pursed and his fists clenched. "I didn't get my wish. Stupid box! I didn't get nothin'. Santa lied."

Benny glanced at Laura whose eyes shined with tears. He sat and pulled Gabe onto his lap, wiping the tears from his eyes. "Santa didn't lie. He just didn't explain how magic works. Sometimes magic needs a little help. Wishing for what you want is the first step in making a plan. I wished for a job, but I still had to go out and find the job that was best for me. Then I wished for someone to love..." His voice trailed off as he looked at Laura, still holding the fruitcake in her hands. "I met Miss Laura and fell in love with her. That's a special kind of magic between two adults."

Laura started to say something, but Benny shook

his head. This wasn't the time or place. They'd be able to talk later. Right now, it was important to make Gabe feel better. "This year I was going to wish for something special, too," he said. "I was going to wish for a family, just like you did."

Gabe's eyes were wide with wonder. "Really? You wanted a family, too?"

"Yes," Benny said. "And I think there's a way we can both get our wishes."

He led Gabe to the couch, then went to Laura and took the fruitcake from her hands and asked her to sit with Gabe. He brought the fruitcake into the kitchen and retrieved the ring box from his dresser.

Returning to the couch, he knelt in front of Laura and opened the box. "I love you, Laura. And if you want a marriage of convenience so we can adopt Gabe, I'll go along with it. I promise to be a good husband to you and a good father to Gabe. I'll work every day to make you love me the way I love you." He held out the ring. "Laura, will you marry me and make me the happiest man on earth?"

Gabe bounced up and down. "Say yes, say yes please!"

Laura looked at the ring, then gazed deep into Benny's eyes. "I don't want a marriage of convenience," she said. "I never did. That was Carol's idea. I want a real marriage, a real husband..." she drew Gabe close, "and yes, a real family. I love you Benny, and I'd love nothing more than to be your wife."

Benny slid the ring onto her finger, his eyes clouded with tears of happiness. He stood and pulled Laura into his arms, holding her close until he could feel her heartbeat.

Gabe stood on the couch and wrapped his arms around both of them. "Me too," he cried. "Me too."

Benny laughed, then turned to Gabe, his face serious. "Gabe, would you do us the honor of being our son?"

"Can I? Really?"

"As soon as we get married, we can file the adoption papers." He turned pleading eyes to Laura, realizing he should have checked with her first.

Gabe followed suit. "Can we, Miss Laura?"

Laura smiled. "Of course," she agreed. "On one condition."

Gabe and Benny both held their breath.

"After the adoption goes through, you can call me *mom*, okay?"

"Mom," he said, trying the word out for size. He looked at Benny. "And Dad?"

Benny nodded.

Gabe pointed to the Christmas box. His eyes filled with wonder. "It really is magic. It granted my one and only wish." He blinked back happy tears. "This is the bestest day of my whole life!"

"Mine too," Benny said, holding them both close. "Mine too."

Epilogue

They rushed the wedding so they could file the adoption papers as soon as possible. A Christmas themed wedding seemed most appropriate, even though it was early January. Nick, dressed in his Santa regalia, performed the ceremony. Who knew that in addition to being an egg farmer and sometimes Santa he was also an ordained minister? Gabe, acting as Benny's best man, stood beside him at the altar.

Carol, Sally, Beverley, Lou, Judy and Ivy, along with several of Laura's bookstore customers and members of the writers' group sat on the bride's side. Benny's family sat on the groom's side. They had all rearranged their flight plans to attend the wedding. Everyone was there to share their special day.

Laura walked down the aisle alone. It was her choice, knowing this was the threshold she'd cross to a lifetime of never being alone again. She was dressed in white lace, holding a bouquet of sunny yellow daisies Benny had special ordered from the florist shop. Benny thought she was the most beautiful bride he'd ever seen and couldn't believe how lucky he was. No, not luck. He finally believed in the power of magic.

Reading from the book, Nick asked, "Who gives this woman…"

"Nobody," Gabe shouted. "We're gonna keep her.

Forever and a half."

Nick smiled. "Fair enough."

"I now pronounce you man, wife…" he looked down at Gabe, "…and son."

Gabe shoved a fist in the air and shouted, "Yahoo!"

Nick chuckled. "I couldn't have said it better."

Sally wiped a tear from her eye. She turned to Lou and said, "I almost feel like they're my own children."

At the reception, Benny asked if he had to give the box back. "Technically I wasn't able to make my last wish."

Nick smiled. "Well, technically both you and Gabe had your wishes granted."

Benny glanced lovingly at his bride and had to agree. There was no need to make any more wishes. He had everything a man could ever need.

He couldn't wait to carry his wife over the threshold to their new home, knowing the magic box would soon be granting wishes to another lucky soul.

A word about the author...

Linda Bleser began her writing career publishing short fiction for women's magazines. She writes heartwarming, powerful, thought-provoking women's fiction novels.

A transplanted New Yorker, Linda and her husband have retired to sunny Florida where she continues to write on the beach or poolside.

Thank you for purchasing
this publication of The Wild Rose Press, Inc.

For questions or more information
contact us at
info@thewildrosepress.com.

The Wild Rose Press, Inc.
www.thewildrosepress.com